W9-CRG-783

Red scrunched into the other backseat beside me, and Joe and Kat started to buckle themselves into the front seats. The engine sputtered and caught, and Uncle Joe revved it a little. "See you," Dad yelled over the roar, and then we were rolling across the bumpy hayfield, gaining speed, the pitch of the engine rising to a frantic whine and the plane's whole frame vibrating in sympathy.

The trees along the side of the field flashed past in a yellow-green blur, but the ones at the end of the field, directly in front of us, just kept getting clearer—and closer.

Suddenly Red's elbow jabbed me in the ribs. "How come you're so pale, Geronimo?" he asked innocently.

I looked at him. He was having the time of his life. To him, this was just as much fun as that double-loop roller coaster. Well, he'd flown a half a dozen times before—in big commercial planes, that is. But for me, this was number one, and I suspected this wasn't breaking into flying the easy eay.

"I'm always pale when my life's in danger," I muttered.

Red laughed. "Don't sweat it, Geronimo. Compared to that maniac horse you ride every day, this is dead safe." He could have picked a better adjective.

MARILYN HALVORSON is the author of *Cowboys Don't Cry*, winner of the Clarke Irwin/Alberta Culture Writing for Youth Competition and a Junior Literary Guild Selection, and *Let It Go*, both available in Laurel-Leaf editions. She lives in Alberta, Canada.

Marie Fletne Memorial Library
49 S. White Horse Pk.
Berlin, NJ 08009

ALSO AVAILABLE IN LAUREL-LEAF BOOKS:

QUANTITY SALES

Most Dell books are available at special quantity dis-counts when purchased in bulk by corporations, organiza-tions, and special-interest groups. Custom imprinting or excerpting can also be done to fit special needs. For details write: Dell Publishing, 666 Fifth Avenue, New York, NY 10103. Attn.: Special Sales Department.

INDIVIDUAL SALES

Are there any Dell books you want but cannot find in your local stores? If so, you can order them directly from us. You can get any Dell book in print. Simply include the book's title, author, and ISBN number if you have it, along with a check or money order (no cash can be accepted) for the full retail price plus $2.00 to cover shipping and handling. Mail to: Dell Readers Service, P.O. Box 5057, Des Plaines, IL 60017.

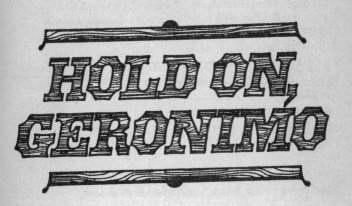

HOLD ON, GERONIMO

Marilyn Halvorson

LAUREL-LEAF BOOKS bring together under a single imprint outstanding works of fiction and nonfiction particularly suitable for young adult readers, both in and out of the classroom. Charles F. Reasoner, Professor Emeritus of Children's Literature and Reading, New York University, is consultant to this series.

Published by
Dell Publishing
a division of
Bantam Doubleday Dell Publishing Group, Inc.
666 Fifth Avenue
New York, New York 10103

This work was first published in Canada by Irwin Publishing Inc. under the title *Nobody Said It Would Be Easy*.

Copyright © 1987 by Marilyn Halvorson

All rights reserved. No part of this book may be reproduced or transmitted in any form or by any means, electronic or mechanical, including photocopying, recording, or by any information storage and retrieval system, without the written permission of the Publisher, except where permitted by law. For information address: Delacorte Press, New York, New York 10103.

The trademark Laurel-Leaf Library® is registered in the U.S. Patent and Trademark Office.

ISBN: 0-440-20409-7

RL: 5.5

Reprinted by arrangement with Delacorte Press

Printed in the United States of America

August 1989

10 9 8 7 6 5 4 3 2

KRI

To the memory of my dad, Trygve Halvorson, who taught me that the things worth doing are never easy.

1

"Okay, doc, make my day," I said, grinning as I held out my arm for him. I'd been waiting for this for so long.

Dr. Meyer gave kind of a disgusted snort. "You keep bouncing around like that, Lance, and what I'm likely to make is a big hole in your hide. Now sit still and quit twitching," he said, cautiously beginning to cut into my cast.

I couldn't wait to scratch under where the cast had been for so long. Not to mention a few other important things—like write notes in school that I could actually read, zip my pants a lot more conveniently, and start drawing again.

The doctor cut through the plaster at last. Now he was working on the padding underneath with a gruesome-looking pair of overgrown scissors. . . .

At last, skin! Dr. Meyer pulled off the last layer of padding, and while he hauled the whole mess off to a garbage can I took a good look. And was kind of disappointed. I'd forgotten that spending a summer not able to do much except let the sun shine on me had left me with a tan like you wouldn't believe. But of course the part under the cast wasn't tanned. It looked white—and kind of scaly from being covered up so long. It reminded me of a lizard's belly—which may look fine on a lizard . . .

I turned my hand over and studied the scar—a long, ugly, pink seam where the knife had slashed across my palm. Would it show up this much forever?

Dr. Meyer had come back and was standing there looking down at my hand too, not saying anything, just looking. I figured he could say *something*. I mean, I read once there's a gorilla somewhere that knows four hundred words. Wouldn't you think a guy who'd made it through medical school could come up with a dozen or two?

"So, how's it look?" I asked, mainly to break the silence. I gave him a grin to cheer him up. "Good as new, huh?" I added, flexing my fingers to prove how well they'd healed. Only—I blinked—my fingers didn't move. It was weird. I knew I was going through the right motions—or trying to, at least. My brain was sending the right messages. Even in ten weeks of not using your right hand you don't forget how it works. But mine *didn't* work.

Then something else struck me. That hand didn't *feel* right either. It was like I was wearing a steel glove—and it was about three sizes too small. Everything felt tight, locked up solid. It had been feeling that way for a while now, I realized. Come on, stupid, I told myself. Your imagination's getting out of control again. That hand's just a little stiff from not using it for so long. It'll work. Try harder. So I tried. I tried until I could see the muscles standing out in my forearm, sweat broke out all over me, and a dull ache began to throb its way through my hand. But my fingers didn't bend.

I could feel the panic starting to rise. No way was I going to fall apart in front of Dr. Meyer's disapproving eyes. But when I looked up at him, it wasn't disapproval I saw on his face. It was more like worry, and something like regret. That's when a big, cold fist started clenching in my guts, and I realized with kind of a shock that I was scared. "It doesn't work," I said. I looked up at Dr. Meyer again. "My hand doesn't work," I repeated, as if I were telling him something he didn't already know.

He gave me sort of a slow nod, but he still didn't say anything and the silence was driving me crazy. Come on, doc, quit stalling. Come up with some answers. "So, what's wrong with it?" I asked out loud. "Why won't my fingers bend? My hand's all healed. It was supposed to be okay when the cast came off . . ."

Dr. Meyer took off his glasses and rubbed his forehead as if he had a headache. He gave me a long look and, when the words finally came, they were worse than the silence. "I didn't promise you that, Lance," he said in a voice that sounded tired. "Nobody said it was going to be that easy."

I sat staring at him, the truth slowly dawning on me. He hadn't been surprised. He'd known all along it was going to be like this. He'd known and he'd let me walk right into it. I started to get mad, and at least the anger felt better than the fear. "Why didn't you tell me?" I demanded. "You knew right from the start, didn't you?"

Dr. Meyer shook his head. "No, Lance," he said wearily. "I didn't *know*. I knew it was a possibility, that's all. The jury doesn't come in on something like this until the cast comes off. There was no point in having you spend the whole summer worrying yourself sick over something that might not even happen."

"So," I said, surprised my voice sounded this calm, "how long before it gets okay again?"

Dr. Meyer hesitated—and I think it was the hesitation that panicked me more than the answer did. "I don't know. It depends on—"

I didn't give him a chance to finish the sentence. "You mean it might be like this forever?" I asked almost in a whisper.

I'll give the doctor credit for one thing. He looked me straight in the eye when he answered. "It's possible," he said slowly, "but there's every reason to . . ."

He might as well have saved his breath. I wasn't listening. I couldn't hear anything but one word echoing through my head. Forever, forever, forever . . .

Hey, this can't be happening to me. Listen, God, you've

got the wrong guy for this. I'm not the type to be a cripple —I could hardly even stand the sound of the word. I haven't got the patience for it. Or the time. I've got a lot of things to do. Horses to break. Calves to rope. I'm gonna rodeo like Dad used to. I've gotta have two good hands for those things.

Then something else hit me. My drawing. The one thing I was *really* good at. That meant something real special to me. I couldn't lose that—could I?

The panic inside me finally broke loose. "No!" I yelled. "It don't depend on nothin'. It's okay. I can close it." And, real fast, the way you rip a piece of tape off a cut so the pain comes and goes before you know it, I reached over with my good hand and tried to force my fingers to close into a fist.

Instantly the pain hit me, a jagged explosion that tore through my hand and sent red-hot lightning bolts all the way to my shoulder. I clenched my teeth on a scream, but it still came out halfway between a groan and a sob. Dr. Meyer grabbed me by the shoulder. "Lance, don't—" he began, but I broke loose from him and stood up, knocking a bunch of stuff off the table beside me.

"Leave me alone!" I yelled at him. "Doctors are supposed to make things better, but you didn't. . . ." I turned away and stood there staring at a chart on the wall but not seeing a thing.

I heard Dr. Meyer stand up behind me and carefully put all the stuff back on the table. Then he turned to me. "All right, cowboy," he said in a tone of voice that got my attention, "that's about enough." He pointed to the chair. "Sit down."

Obediently, I sank into the chair. Dr. Meyer was looking at me. I could feel it, but I wouldn't look up. "Did that make you feel any better?" he asked at last.

Slowly I looked up and shook my head. "No," I said miserably, feeling like a real jerk.

"I didn't think so," Dr. Meyer said, his face relaxing into

almost a hint of a smile. He sat down absent-mindedly, drew a few doodles on his prescription pad, and then started talking again. "I don't blame you for being upset," he said. "Maybe it wasn't fair not to prepare you for this possibility. But it's a little late to kick that one around now. Things are the way they are, and you can't change them. What you can do is decide how you're going to handle them. The way I see it, you've got three choices. You can sit around and feel sorry for yourself." I'm working on that one right now, I thought to myself. "Or, you can react like you did a minute ago, panic like a wild animal in a trap and tear yourself up a little more." No, once was enough for that one. "Or, you could try growing up a little." He gave me a look that told me he figured I had a ways to go in that department. "Accept things the way they are for now"—he stressed those last two words— "and work on making them better."

He paused there and looked at me as if he expected an answer. But I was still waiting for choice number four. On multiple-choice tests at school, it's usually "None of the above," and right now that was the one I was planning to pick. . . . I just sat there looking at him and he started talking again. "It's not as bad as you're letting yourself think," he went on reassuringly; "with a little time and a good therapy program, there's a fairly decent chance you'll regain full function in that hand yet."

That was supposed to make me feel a whole lot better, I guess. And maybe it would have—if I'd been listening. Oh, I was hearing the words, all right. They were running through my head in a steady stream but that's just what they were like, a stream of water running over rocks, making a lot of sound but not meaning a thing. My ears were hearing, but my mind wasn't taking it in.

Vaguely, I noticed that Dr. Meyer had stopped talking and picked up the phone. Then he said something, but it didn't register. I just kept staring at my hand. Dr. Meyer raised his voice. "Lance," he repeated, "what's your phone number?" I stared at him, wondering why he wanted to know. He couldn't phone me. I was here.

"It's 555-2156," I said.

He dialed, waited, listened. After a while he hung up. "Do you know where your dad is, Lance?" he asked.

I shook my head. "He's hardly ever in the house," I said, somehow glad that Dr. Meyer hadn't gotten him. I wasn't sure why, but I didn't really want him talking to Dad.

The doctor sighed, wrote a few lines on a piece of paper, and handed it to me. I took it. I didn't know what it was, and I didn't care. I just wanted out of there. "Give that to your dad. It's important."

"Sure," I muttered and stuffed the paper in my shirt pocket without looking at it. I bet it was important. I could just see it: Dear Mr. Ducharme, Your son has an attitude problem. He is not adjusting well to his handicap.

Dr. Meyer must have been a pretty fair mind reader because he sighed and gave me a tired look. "You're waiting for me to give you the guarantee, aren't you, Lance? You think this should be like installing a new muffler and sending you home with a promise of your money back if it turns out defective. But, unfortunately, people aren't that easy. I can't promise you what I don't know. You could be using that hand in a week, or you might never use it. There are many aspects of healing that we don't understand. It's as much a mental process as a physical one. . . ." I guess about then he realized he'd been going on for a long time without getting any response from me. "Do you understand what I'm trying to tell you, Lance?"

The truth was I wasn't trying very hard. "Not really," I said, not able to keep the bitterness from edging into my voice. "Unless you're tryin' to say that all I have to do is wish for it and my fairy godmother will make everything all right."

I was just being mouthy, and I knew it. If Dr. Meyer had

gotten mad at me, I would have deserved it. But he didn't. Instead he nodded and said, completely serious, "That's closer than you think." He gave me a long look. "You may not believe this, but I'd stake thirty years of medical practice on the idea that regaining the use of that hand really depends on one thing . . ."

He waited, and I knew I was supposed to get curious and ask. I was curious—but I wouldn't ask. So he told me anyhow. "It depends on how badly you want it."

2

I guess I must have walked the six blocks back to school on autopilot because I sure can't remember a thing about them. All I could think about was what Dr. Meyer had said. That last sentence kept playing over and over in my mind: "It depends on how badly you want it." I even knew he might be right. Thinking you can do something has a lot of power sometimes. I knew it worked with horses. You get on a green bronc giving off scared vibes, and he'll most likely toss you into the next county. But get on him thinking you can ride him, and chances are you can bluff him into believing it and behaving himself.

But what Dr. Meyer was talking about was a lot more personal than breaking horses. Wanting something that much meant committing yourself completely. It was like leaning way out across a canyon to reach somebody who'll pull you across to the other side. But what if nobody's there to grab you?

I'd wanted something the way Dr. Meyer was talking about only once before in my life. A long time ago. When I was five years old. That was the year my mom left. I'd wanted her to come back so bad. And I was so sure she would. I'd leaned out a long way reaching for her, but she wasn't there. She didn't come back. Not until last spring. Ten years was too long for me to wait, and when she did come it set off a whole chain of events that left me so mixed up I still wasn't sure if I was glad or sorry she was even alive.

One thing I did know, though. I was scared to ever want anything that bad again.

I turned a corner and, suddenly, I was back at the school. The parking lot was full of buses, I noticed kind of vaguely, my mind still a long ways from the rest of me. I looked at my watch. 3:08. School was out already. And the buses, especially our bus, pulled out at 3:10 on the dot. I started to run but, sure enough, just as I came tearing into the parking lot, the bus started to pull out. I made it in, though, and almost to my seat. Then the bus took off with a jerk that landed me in the seat—and almost in Red Cantrell's lap. He looked up at me. "Nice of you to drop in, Lance," he said, straight-faced, as he gathered up the pile of books I'd landed on. "So," he went on innocently—not that Red's got an innocent bone in his body— "how *were* things down at the poolhall?" He knew exactly where I'd been, and why, but Red wouldn't pass up a chance to bug me a little. Red and I have been best friends for a long time, but we're still always hassling each other. I guess that's *because* we're friends. Come to think of it, I'm a lot more polite to my enemies.

"You want to be the first person to get off this bus through the ceiling?" I asked him pleasantly, while gripping him firmly by the throat with my good hand. I could feel myself starting to relax. Life was falling back into its normal pattern, and what had happened at the doctor's office was beginning to seem like a bad dream.

"Okay, okay, I get the picture," Red squeaked airlessly, and I let go. Then he turned serious—and I wished he hadn't. "So you got it off," he said. "Let's see."

I'd been expecting that. Red's real interested in anything to do with what makes people tick. I mean, the guy is so deranged that he actually *likes* biology class.

I hesitated. "The hand, Geronimo. Let's see how it looks," Red repeated patiently.

Reluctantly, I held it out. He looked it over.

"Pretty, huh?" I said, sourly.

9

Red shrugged. "I've seen worse," he said, and I didn't bother asking where. "So how's it feel?" he asked, grinning.

"Okay," I lied, but that didn't discourage him from asking the next question. "How's it work? Good as new, huh?"

I didn't say anything for a minute. I could feel my stomach knotting up again. I didn't want to talk about it right now. But if anyone had a right to know, it was Red. He'd been there when it all happened. Red had driven me to the hospital, got me there while I still had some blood left in me. "Yeah," I heard myself say, "It'll be okay. I'm just not supposed to use it much for a while." I didn't need to lie to my best friend. But it was weird. Like I was ashamed to tell him the truth. Like having something physically wrong with me was a disgrace.

"Yeah?" Red said, interested. "How long's a while? What did the doctor say about—"

"Nothin' much," I said, cutting him off. "Drop the third degree, huh?"

Red gave me a look that said plenty, but he didn't ask any more questions. He's the kind of guy you don't have to draw pictures for.

He turned away and started sorting out a big pile of books. Then he dumped them in my lap. "Okay, Geronimo, since you're already in such a great mood, this ought to finish making your day. I picked up your homework for you."

"Thanks a lot, buddy," I said sarcastically, sorting through the pile. They were all there—biology, math, social studies, and another book I'd never seen before. "Hey," I said, "this one's not mine."

" 'Fraid it is now, Geronimo. Mr. Cartland handed them out this afternoon after you left."

"But I've already got an English text."

"Not this one, you haven't," he announced, picking up

the book and pointing to the title. "You are about to meet Shakespeare. *Hamlet,* to be specific."

"*Hamlet*? That's a book? Sounds more like something rich people eat for breakfast."

Red sighed. "Geronimo," he said, trying to sound serious and cultured, "*you* are talking about an omelette. *I* am talking about the Prince of Denmark."

"Yeah? Who's he? A Scandinavian rock singer?"

Red gave up. "Figure it out for yourself, genius. We're supposed to read the first act for homework."

I groaned, opened the book and read a couple of lines—and almost passed out. I mean, school may not be my strong point, but I don't have a reading problem. I usually go through a book every week or two with no trouble. Looking at this, though, I had a sinking feeling that William Shakespeare didn't ride the same trails as Louis L'Amour and Max Brand. I couldn't even pronounce the names of the guys in this book, let alone figure out what they were talking about. "Red," I said weakly, "is this written in English?"

Red laughed. "Man, is Mr. Cartland going to enjoy teaching you Shakespeare!" he said, shaking his head.

"Not half as much as I'm going to enjoy learning it," I muttered. "Anyhow, if we have to read Shakespeare why couldn't he have picked something I understand. I kind of liked *Romeo and Juliet* with those rival gangs feuding and the two kids killing themselves for true love. That whole thing ended up with more bodies lying around than a *Conan the Barbarian* movie—"

Before I could finish, Red cut me off. "Geronimo," he said, "you don't want to see a grown man cry, do you?" Before I could say, depends who, he added, "Then don't ever try that line on Mr. Cartland." We both started to laugh.

Red turned half serious. "You didn't actually *read Romeo and Juliet*, did you?" he asked in a puzzled tone.

"Sure," I said straight-faced. "How else would I know all that stuff?"

Red's puzzled frown got deeper. I weakened. "Well, actually the movie was on *The Late Show* once," I admitted. "Red, you should have *seen* that Juliet. She was—"

"Shut up, Shakespeare, and get off the bus." We had come to a grinding stop at my gate. As I stood up, Red asked, "We gonna get together for a while tonight?"

I hesitated. Just being with Red these few minutes on the bus had improved my mood a whole lot. When I was clowning around with him, I didn't have to think. But the other side of it was that I *needed* to do some thinking to try to get control of this hand business. Just pretending this afternoon had never happened was fine for a fifteen-minute bus ride. But I knew it wasn't going to work for long.

I ran out of time to decide. I shrugged and started down the aisle. "Yeah, sure," I said. "I'll check and see if Dad needs me to do anything; then I'll give you a call."

"Okay. See ya."

"See ya, Paleface."

3

The bus rumbled away in a cloud of diesel smoke, and I breathed a sigh of relief. The weekend. Two whole days of having everybody off my case. Suddenly I couldn't wait to get up to the house, dump my books, get into some decently dirty clothes, and start living again. I broke into a run.

I was halfway up the long lane that led to the ranch buildings when I first noticed the horse and rider way over on the other side of the pasture. Dad must be working out one of the three-year-olds he was breaking. I stopped to watch. He was really putting that horse through its paces—galloping in big circles, doing figure eights and sliding stops and rollbacks—the works. That horse could do it all, I thought admiringly. Dad must have been putting in a lot of time on those horses. None of them had looked that good last time I'd seen him ride them. He was riding great too. Like a part of the horse, the two of them out there tearing holes in the wind.

That was what I needed. To get out there in the wind and the sun and ride and ride—leave everything else behind. I wouldn't bother changing my clothes. These would get decently dirty soon enough anyhow. I dumped my books, even His Royal Highness, the Prince, in a heap at the edge of the lane and took off for the barn at a run.

I grabbed a halter out of the tack room and was just climbing over the pasture fence when the horse and rider caught my eye again. A lot closer now—and headed this way at a dead run. That was kind of weird. Dad didn't usually ride that fast without a good reason. I wondered if something was wrong. I sat there for a minute, on the top rail, watching the sun reflect off the horse's fire-red hide. Then, all of a sudden, something clicked. That wasn't one of the three-year-olds out there. There was only one horse on the place that color. My horse. Spider. Nobody rode Spider but me.

That *wasn't* Dad on him. I could see that for sure as the horse and rider got closer. But who else could it be? Somebody with a lot of long, black hair streaming out behind in the wind. A girl! A girl I'd never even seen before riding hell-bent-for-leather across the pasture on *my* horse. Something pretty strange was going on here and I didn't like it. Whoever she was, she was going to get her neck broke. And, the mood I was in, if the horse didn't do it for her, I just might.

I jumped off the fence and started walking out to meet them. The distance between us was narrowing fast now, but Spider wasn't slowing down. He was coming straight at me like an out-of-control freight train on a downhill stretch. The girl wasn't even trying to slow him down. Just the opposite. She was leaning forward, low on his neck, and riding him like a jockey bringing a winner down the homestretch. And—I couldn't believe this—she was riding him *bareback.* Even I never rode Spider bareback if there was any way of getting around it.

I stopped walking and just stood there in her path to make her rein in—which she didn't. Horse and rider kept closing in on me at a dead gallop. They were real close now. I could see Spider's nostrils flaring red with excitement. I could see the whites of his eyes. And I could see hoofprints across my chest in about half a second if she didn't stop that horse or I didn't get out of there.

Then I saw the look on her face. She was grinning—a big,

sassy grin that had "I dare you to stand there" written all over it. That did it. I wouldn't have moved if it *had* been a freight train barreling toward me.

Spider's hoofbeats were shaking the ground when, in the last possible split second, she reined him hard to the right and brought him around in a circle. He collected himself and when, at last, she pulled him in, he slid to a perfect roping-horse stop right beside me. The girl looked down at me. She was laughing. "Nerves of steel, huh, Lance? Well, you always did have more guts than brains."

I stared at her. "Yeah? Well, anybody who pulls what you just did hasn't got *any* brains! What do you think you're doin' anyhow?" I yelled, so mad I was practically shaking. And *who* are you? I wanted to yell that at her too, but I didn't. Because, if she knew me, I must be supposed to know her too, and no way was I about to give her the satisfaction of finding out I didn't have a clue who she was.

The fact that I was almost spitting nails didn't seem to worry her a whole lot. She ignored my question and leaned down to pat Spider's neck. "He's a lot of horse," she said admiringly. "Does he belong to your dad or is he one of Frank's?"

"Neither one." I spat out the words like January icicles. "He belongs to *me*. And who said you could ride him?"

She shrugged, unconcerned. "Nobody," she said. "I just came out, looked the horses over, and picked the best one." She grinned and added, "But nobody said I *couldn't* ride him."

That didn't strike me as funny. "Well, I'm sayin' it right now. Get off my horse before you get hurt."

She laughed. "Before I *what?*" she said. "Come on, Lance. Get serious. Do I look like I'm gonna get hurt?"

Well, the truth was that anybody who could ride like I'd just seen her ride wasn't in much danger of getting hurt on *any* horse. But that didn't do a thing toward cooling my temper down.

"Yeah," I said, the anger spilling into my voice, "you look like you're gonna get hurt right now." Before she had time to react, I reached up with my left hand, grabbed her arm, and hauled her off Spider's back.

The instant her feet touched the ground she spun around to face me. Her hand came up so fast I was sure she was going to hit me. I think that idea did cross her mind, but she didn't do it. Instead she swept her hand across her forehead and pushed that long, tangled hair back out of her eyes. And one look at those eyes knocked the wind out of me faster than a punch in the stomach would have. I'd been expecting them to be dark—to match the black hair and deep tan skin—but they weren't. Rimmed by thick, dark lashes that only made their color more startling, they were the stormiest pair of thundercloud-blue eyes I'd ever seen —except once.

Four years is a long time, especially when you're a kid growing up, and a lot of things had changed since I'd seen her. But not those eyes. They made it seem only yesterday that I'd first met Kat. My cousin. No. Actually, stepcousin. No way would I unnecessarily take the blame for having her for a blood-relative. She was my Uncle Joe's stepdaughter, and her full name was Kathleen Annette Teresa Ducharme. I tried calling her that once. Just once. She hit me so hard it made my lip bleed. Nothing suited her better than "Kat" did, anyhow. She was all claws and curiosity.

But what was she doing here? She was supposed to be at home, way up north, past Fort St. John, a nice, safe five hundred miles or so away from me. I took a quick look around. No, unless I was going blind, there weren't any extra vehicles parked in the yard.

Why hadn't I recognized her sooner? That was what was really bugging me. I'd spent two weeks with her when Dad and I went up there to visit four years ago, and I would have sworn that everything about her was permanently burned into my nightmares.

I returned her hostile stare, and slowly the answer formed in my mind. Kat had changed. She had changed a whole lot. In fact, the eyes were about the only thing I could even associate with the memory of the ten-year-old savage who'd dropped a rotten magpie egg down my back. In that memory, she was a pudgy little kid with a big wad of pink bubble gum in her mouth and spruce needles tangled in her hair. A grubby, homely brat with the looks of a Cabbage Patch Kid and the disposition of a wolverine.

Well, I decided, still staring, she didn't look like a Cabbage Patch Kid now. Not by a long shot. I guess she hadn't really lost all that much weight. Rearranged, would be more like it. And I liked the new arrangement a whole lot better. That is, on any girl but Kat, I would have liked it a whole lot. When it came to her though, I figured that, in any disguise, she was still the same old Kat—which is the only way I knew to spell "trouble" with three letters.

"Hey, come on, Macho Mouse, get off my case. I didn't hurt your prize horse any, did I?" she snapped, her eyes flashing. I felt almost relieved. Whatever she looked like on the outside, Kat hadn't really changed.

I took a deep breath and counted to about a hundred and ten before I dared say anything more to her. How does she do it? I wondered. She comes into my territory, takes my horse without asking, practically tramples me into the ground with him, and then manages to get *me* on the defensive.

"That's not the point, Kat," I said at last, doing my best not to get mad again. "Spider used to be a rodeo bronc. He's real unpredictable. He could start bucking again anytime. It took two years for me to get him so I could ride him. Nobody else rides him. He's dangerous, Kat. Can't you get that through your head?"

That was the moment Spider picked to lay his head against Kat's shoulder and half-close his eyes. He looked like he might roll over and wag his tail any minute. Kat reached over and scratched him behind the ears. "Right, Lance," she said. "Real dangerous." She laughed.

I glared at Spider. You four-legged traitor, I thought. And to think I saved you from the dog-food factory.

4

That time we'd spent together back in the summer before sixth grade hadn't been a visit. It had been a war. Thinking back on it now, I wonder why our parents didn't knock our heads together and lock us in the cellar till we grew up. The two of us just wouldn't quit. Everything had been a competition, a challenge to see who would come out ahead.

At first, I'd tried playing by the rules—the ones that say girls aren't as tough as guys, so you have to give them a few breaks. The problem was that Kat didn't play by any rules. Every time I tried to give her a break, I ended up getting broken. So finally I gave up and started playing to win—and I still didn't do much more than come out even.

We did everything—raced each other to the top of fifty-foot trees; caught Uncle Joe's unbroken two-year-old colts and played rodeo; made bows and arrows and pretended we were Indians (which wasn't hard, since we really were part Indian) had raft races down the river on homemade rafts that fell apart in the middle of the race. Uncle Joe made us quit that—Kat had just casually forgot to mention that she couldn't swim.

And then we dared each other. As long as I live, I'll never forget the big hornet's nest. A gray "paper" one, big around as a basketball, and hanging just at eye level from a poplar branch. Kat and I must have sat there on a log for an hour, just looking at it. Watching those big black-striped hornets buzz in and out. Finally Kat turned to look at me.

"Wonder what they'd do if somebody stuffed something in that hole and blocked it up so they couldn't get out," she said, supercasual.

I thought the answer was pretty obvious. "They'd get real mad," I said.

"Think so?"

"I know so."

Those blue eyes narrowed dangerously. "Bet you haven't got the guts to sneak up there and shove this stick in that hole," she challenged, lazily holding out a piece of dry branch.

Well, in the first place, I was a fairly bright kid. And in the second place, hornets were one notch higher than grizzly bears on my list of critters not to mess with. But in the third place . . .

"Oh yeah? Give me that stick."

Everything went fine until the last second when I was real close to the nest and one of those big honkers started circling my ear, buzzing like a chain saw and flying like a kamikaze pilot. I panicked, jammed the stick in too hard, and knocked the whole mess onto the ground.

I got stung seven times—my ex-lucky number—including twice on my lip, had to live on soup for three days, and, for some reason, got absolutely no sympathy from anybody.

But a few battle wounds didn't keep me from plotting my revenge. The next day I bet Kat she couldn't ride Uncle Joe's old Jersey milk cow. Well, good old Brownie turned out to be pretty athletic for a cow. She took off running and bucking like a wild Brahma and headed straight for the water trough. Of course, being too good a rider to fall off and too stupid to bail out, Kat was still with Brownie when she bounced to a stiff-legged stop right at the edge of the trough. Kat flew over her head, landed in the trough, half knocked herself out, and darn near drowned before I could drag her out of there.

* * *

Maybe this was what growing up did, I thought. Changed the yelling matches into silent staring contests. I wondered how Kat was seeing me now. Had I changed as much as she had? I doubted it.

But of all the stuff I was wondering about, there was one question that had me so curious I was going to have to break down and ask. I took one more glance around the yard just to make sure I hadn't missed anything. Kat's eyes followed my gaze. "Lose somethin'?" she asked, her voice taking on that old, familiar, "I-know-something-you-don't-know" tone.

I ignored her attitude and asked my question. "How'd you get here anyway?"

She tossed her hair out of her eyes and gave me her sassy grin. Right away, I knew I wasn't going to get a straight answer. "Well," she said, mysteriously, "you might say I just dropped out of the sky—you know, like an angel."

In spite of the mood I was in, I couldn't help but grin a little. "Kat," I said, "if you dropped out of the sky with wings and a halo, singin' the 'Hallelujah Chorus,' you'd still be no angel."

Kat gave me a haughty look, as if I were a worm who had dared to speak. Then she nodded toward the hayfield behind me. "You're lookin' in the wrong direction," she said. I turned around and there, sitting on the edge of the field, sagging like a dying duck, was Uncle Joe's old Cessna-180. The last time I'd seen her I was sure there was nothing but copper wire and Crazy Glue holding her together, and four years of rough bush-flying hadn't done anything to change my opinion. "You and Uncle Joe flew all the way down here in *that*?"

"And just exactly what is wrong with *The Falcon*?" she demanded.

The Falcon? For a second, my mind was blank. And then I

remembered. *"The Millennium Falcon,"* I said softly, thinking out loud.

Kat nodded and she smiled, not sassy this time but softer and more daydreamy. "Yeah," she said. "It's still on there, you know."

"No kiddin'? That must've been pretty good paint we found." I caught myself smiling too. It seemed like *The Falcon* had always been sort of a charm, the only thing that could bring a truce between me and Kat. The one and only time the two of us had ever gotten along, come pretty close to being friends, even, was the day we'd painted *The Falcon* together.

Kat restlessly scuffed patterns in the dirt with the toe of her boot. She looked up and gave me a jolt with the eyes. "So," she demanded, "are we gonna just stand around here all day, or are we gonna do something?"

Now there was a real good question, I thought tiredly. Of all the times in my life for Kat to show up, this had to be the worst. I still hadn't gotten over the shock of finding out about my hand, and my brain felt so overloaded I thought it was going to start blowing circuits. All I wanted was a chance to be alone for a while to try to get my life straightened out. And what do I get? The one person in the whole world totally guaranteed to finish messing up my mind.

One thing for sure, though. Kat was here in the flesh, and not about to be wished away. The only way she was leaving was when *The Falcon* flew. Until then, I was stuck with her. But that didn't mean I had to enjoy it. And right then Kat spotted the Saint Christopher's medal that I wore on a chain around my neck.

"What's that?" she asked.

"What's it look like?" I snapped.

She just shrugged and I thought the subject was closed. I should have known better.

"Get it from your girlfriend?" she asked, with a wicked grin.

"Not exactly." I muttered, turning away. "I'm goin' ridin'. Guess you can come with me," I added reluctantly. Then, just to rattle her chain a little, I threw in, "We got a tame horse we keep for girls to ride."

5

We started toward the barn. Kat still had hold of Spider's reins, and really I should have just let her take him in. But as I said before, with Kat I never do the reasonable thing.

"Give me my horse," I said stubbornly, being careful to hold out my left hand for the reins. Kat hesitated, but she didn't say anything. She just slapped the reins into my hand a little harder than I thought was necessary and kept on walking. Spider started to follow her, so I gave the reins a little pull to let him know he was with me now. He stepped over obediently enough, but I swear that if a horse can look disappointed, he did. I looked at him, all sweated up and still puffing a little. Sucker! I thought. You've been rode hard and put away wet, and you're still in love with her.

At the pasture gate I automatically dropped Spider's reins so I could reach over and undo the latch with my left hand. And that was one move I shouldn't have made. Because, sure enough, Kat noticed. "Hey, what's wrong with your other hand?" she asked, real interested.

Interest in that hand, especially *her* interest, was something I didn't need. "Aw, nothin' much," I said with a shrug, managing to keep my voice fairly cool and bored-sounding. Maybe she'd just let it go.

But when Kat gets something on her mind, she's just like a yappy little dog that's got hold of a bone and isn't about to let go, no matter what. She just keeps gnawing away at it, and anyone who tries to take it away from her is liable to get bit.

Before I knew what was happening, she'd reached over and grabbed my wrist. "Wow! It sure doesn't look like nothin'," she said, staring at that scar like she'd just discovered an archaeological treasure.

Angrily, I jerked my hand away. "I said it's nothin'!" I yelled, and right away I regretted letting her get to me so easy again.

Kat gave me a disdainful look. "Okay, so it's nothin'," she said with a shrug. "Then how come you're so self-conscious about it? I doubt that's the first scar you ever had."

I doubted it too. Kat knew about at least one—the groove that long-horned cow had made down my ribs that summer in Fort St. John. I can't totally blame it on Kat. All she'd done was dare me to play matador and lend me her jacket for a cape. The cow did the rest. I've gotten cut up plenty of other times too. I think every ax, jackknife, and piece of barbed wire on the place has attacked me at least once. I've got so many old scars on me I look like Rambo—give or take a few muscles, that is.

The knife scar was different though. It was all tied up with a lot of other stuff I wasn't sure I could handle. Fear of not ever using that hand again was the biggest thing. But it wasn't just that. There were the reminders of a few weeks in my life that I'd messed up so bad I'd just like to pretend they never happened. But then I never would have gotten to know my mom again, and I don't want to forget her—at least, most of the time I don't. I guess I'm still so mixed up about everything that happened last spring that I couldn't begin to explain it to my best friend—let alone to my worst enemy. But *she* sure wasn't about to drop the subject.

"So come on Lance. What'd you do this time? Try holding the stick with one hand and chopping kindling with the other?" I didn't say anything, but Kat came up with her own answer anyway. "No, that would have been your left hand. Stop being so mysterious and tell me what happened," she demanded, her patience running out.

Kat not getting her own way is kind of an interesting sight. Sort of like waiting for Old Faithful to blow sky-high. But there was no way I was about to tell her. I led Spider through the gate. "Curiosity killed the Kat," I said over my shoulder and grinned just to irritate her a little more. "Well, you comin' through the gate or not? If you're ridin' with me, you better hurry up." I thought maybe changing the subject might work. It did—for a second. She came through, I shut it, and we started toward the barn. And then she had to start up again.

"But how come it's such a big secret? Did you get in a knife fight or something? Switchblades at dawn and all that stuff?" I could tell she thought that idea was about as far-out as she could get. But in reality, she had hit too close to the truth for it to be funny, and the words touched a nerve already rubbed raw. What little was left of my patience exploded in a flash of pure fury. I swung around and looked her square in the eye. "Yeah," I said in a voice that sounded like it belonged to a stranger.

"Yeah, what?"

"Yeah, you got it. A knife fight. That's how I got cut," I said, taking pleasure in watching her eyes widen.

"Honest?" she asked. Her voice was sort of hushed, and I couldn't tell if she was shocked or impressed. "Tell me the whole story." Okay, I thought, still tense with anger. If she wanted the whole story, she was going to get it—and I hoped it would knock her socks off.

"The fight was with this guy I know who deals a little dope," I began, watching for her reaction. "I was sellin' some stuff for him and, well, some things went wrong, and the deal went sour. He got all freaked out about it—he was so high he didn't know what he was doin' anyhow—and the next thing I know he's wavin' this blade around. I figured somebody was gonna get hurt pretty soon, so I jumped him and took the knife. And that's when I got cut." I paused to let it all sink in. Then, "Okay," I said, my voice cold, "you got the whole story. Feel better now?"

It was one of the few times in her life that Kat didn't have anything to say. She just stared at me like I was some kind of alien. I didn't really blame her for that. Because I could barely recognize me either. Not as the guy in the story I'd just told her, anyway.

I wish I could say that I lied to her. But I hadn't. What I'd told her was the absolute truth. I could have sworn to it in court—I already had, in fact, last month when they called me and Red for witnesses at Randy's trial. Still, in every way that counted, I *had* lied to her. Because of the way I'd made it sound. Like I was proud of the whole thing, or something. And because of what I *hadn't* told her. Like the fact that the deal with Randy had been the first—and I planned on it being the last—time I'd gotten mixed up in the drug scene. And that the only reason I'd done it then was because I was so messed up and mad at the world and trying to find a way to hurt myself and everyone else that counted.

"You deal drugs?" Kat asked at last, and for once her voice didn't hold a challenge. The sassy grin was gone, and it was hard to describe the way she looked. Younger. Dead serious and sort of innocent. Like a little kid who's just asked you if there really is a Santa Claus—but doesn't want to hear the answer.

The silence hung between us for a few more seconds. And then it was too late. Now it would sound as if I were making excuses. Kat was still staring at me, and now I could read what was in her eyes. Disappointment. And that bothered me.

Suddenly I was mad at her all over again. Why did she have to corner me like this? But the anger boiling up inside me wasn't really for her. It was for me. For all the dumb things I'd done to mess up my life. Even as the words came out, I knew it. But knowing it didn't stop me. "Yeah, that's what I said. I was sellin' some grass," I told her, my voice cool and tough. "So what? That's no big deal. Or can't you handle it? Come on, Kat, grow up. You ain't in Fort St. John now."

She looked like I'd hit her. I might as well have. It wouldn't have taken any less class than saying what I did. There had been a time when Kat would have hit *me* for what I'd said too. But I guess she must have left hitting me behind—along with being eleven and ugly. Now she just swallowed and said, real quiet, "No, I guess I can't handle that," and started walking away.

I stood there and watched her and wondered how it was possible for me to be so stupid. I knew I should say I was sorry—and I also knew I wouldn't.

"Hey," I burst out at last, "don't you want to go ridin'?"

She threw me one glance over her shoulder, and it almost froze me. "In Fort St. John," she said, "I don't ride with two-bit hoods." She kept walking.

6

By now I didn't much care if I rode or not, but I went anyway, just to get out of there. For a while I let Spider pick his own trail, but he was sure no ball of fire. I knew he was a long ways from tired, but he'd used up all his flashy moves showing off for Kat, and now he let me know he'd rather be at home eating clover. Too bad, Spider, I thought, nudging him into a reluctant lope. Things are tough all over.

I headed him up the trail toward the beaver dams. I like it up there, especially when I want to get away from the rest of the world. It's real peaceful and, with all the trees turned September-gold, it was pretty too. There was one beaver swimming around in the big dam. I was sure he heard us coming, but he didn't pay any attention till I reined Spider in and eased him right up along the edge of the dam. Then, all of a sudden, that beaver gave his tail a slap that spooked Spider sky-high and almost convinced him to go right back to being a bucking horse. I pulled his head up and settled him back to earth. Then I looked at the spot where the beaver had been. All I expected to see was ripples. But that ornery little critter hadn't even dived. He was still just swimming around, cool as could be. He turned his head a little, and I swear he looked me right in the eye, and then he slapped that tail again. Same reaction from Spider.

We went through that routine two more times, and I was beginning to think I could see the beaver giving me a yellow-toothed grin between slaps. He had to be the most arrogant animal I'd ever run across.

Suddenly it occurred to me to check the time. Almost six o'clock! I hadn't planned to be gone this long. Now, on top of all my other problems, I was going to be late for supper. I pointed Spider toward home, which improved his attitude considerably, touched him with my heels, and we burned up some trail.

I was still late. When I opened the door, the smell of Dad's homemade pork and beans reached out and practically dragged me into the kitchen. It suddenly struck me that I hadn't eaten for more than six hours. For me, that's some kind of record.

But at the sight of Dad and Uncle Joe—and Kat—all sitting there watching me make my grand entrance, I started to lose my appetite. Kat wasted only one glance on me, but it was enough. It made me feel like I'd walked too close to a flamethrower. Okay, if that was the way she wanted it. I threw her back some visual fireworks and turned my attention to Uncle Joe.

One look at him was enough to get anybody's attention. I'd always thought of my dad as being a pretty big man, but Uncle Joe was bigger. Heavier, anyway. He was built about right to be a slightly out-of-shape heavyweight wrestler. And if his body didn't make you stop and take notice, his face would. With that big, black beard and hair that hung in curls to his shoulders, it was like you were looking at the last of the half-tame mountain men. That was exactly the way Joe wanted it. Looking that way was good for his guide and outfitting business. "Them big-city boys come up here figurin' it's the last frontier. Nothin' but wild animals and wilder people. So," and he'd winked and given me a wicked grin, "I do my best not to disappoint them. I meet 'em at the airport, lookin' like I'm all wild and furry and full of fleas, and I say, "Howdy, I'm your guide"; and right away they're happy, knowin' they're gettin' their money's worth of the wild West." He'd paused and rubbed his beard thoughtfully. "At least the ones that don't climb right back on the next plane and take their scalps back home while they still can."

Well, there might have been some truth in that story, but the real truth was that Uncle Joe just happened to like looking the way he did—and if anybody else didn't happen to like it, that was their problem.

If Uncle Joe had noticed that there was a lot of tension hanging in the room, he sure wasn't about to let it interfere with his supper. He looked up and grinned at me. "Well, at last, if it isn't the late, great Lance. How you doin' anyhow, kid?" he boomed in a voice that likely spooked the horses on the next ranch. He stood up, pushed back his chair and grabbed me in a rib-crunching hug. If this was affection, I hoped I'd never get him mad at me. Then he pushed me back to arm's length and looked me over. "Hey," he said, grinning like a well-fed alligator, "what happened to the funny-lookin' short kid that used to live here?" He waited long enough to get me off guard and then added, "You're not short anymore." He laughed. "Oh well, fifty percent ain't bad." He sized me up some more and then turned semiserious. "You really are all growed up, aren't you?"

I wasn't sure how I was supposed to answer a question like that, so I didn't—at least not out loud. But I was thinking about how getting tall and growing up didn't have much to do with each other.

"Looks like you've grown some too," I said, since I couldn't resist getting even. He'd always been on the heavyset side, but since I'd last seen him it seemed like his chest had slid down to where it was hanging over his belt buckle a little. Uncle Joe's eyes followed my gaze and then, before I could duck, he gave me a cuff on the ear. "Mind your manners, child," he chuckled. "Sit down and eat your beans." He spooned a huge helping onto my plate and then refilled his own.

My dad's homemade beans beat anything I've tasted anywhere, but tonight I wasn't enjoying them as much as usual. Not with Kat sitting across the table alternating between shooting poison-tipped looks in my direction and refusing to look at me at all. And anyhow, eating took too much concentration to be fun. Even though I'd had enough practice to be able to handle a fork pretty efficiently left-handed, it still felt awkward. It also felt like Kat was noticing every move I made.

Then the phone rang—and I was out of my chair and halfway through the hall on the first ring. "I'll get it!" I yelled over my shoulder. I didn't know who it was, but a chance to escape was worth the gamble.

It was Red. "Hey, Geronimo, *you* were supposed to phone *me*, remember? I've been sittin' here waitin' half the night," he said, accusingly.

"Oh, yeah, sorry about that. Things have been kinda busy around here." Then, "Hey," I said, feeling just like I figured General Custer would have felt if he'd seen reinforcements come riding over the hill at Little Big Horn, "why don't you come over right away? Dad mentioned something yesterday about the cows on the west quarter needin' salt. We can run some out tonight."

"Yeah, okay, I'. be there in a while."

"Unh-unh. Not a while. Right now."

"What's the big hurry? Those cows gonna die of salt deficiency in the next ten minutes?"

"Skip the humor. Just hurry up. I need you for protection."

"Protection from what?"

"My cousin."

"Oh," Red hesitated. "Well, if you've got company, maybe I'd better not . . ."

"Red . . ." I said threateningly.

"Okay, okay, I'm comin'." Then he added, "Your cousin

must be one tough dude," and I could tell I had him curious.

"Yeah, you might say that," I said. Then I hung up.

By the time I got off the phone, everyone had finished eating and disappeared outside. I took one look at what was left of my plateful of cold beans and contributed them to Tomte, the cat. I glanced out the kitchen window and saw Dad and Uncle Joe sauntering off toward the corral, but Kat was nowhere in sight. Good. I hoped she stayed that way. Then Red and I could just load up a few blocks of salt and take off.

I had a few minutes to kill waiting for Red, so I thought maybe I'd break a record and do a little of that big pile of homework he'd so generously gathered up for me. And that thought led me to another. My homework still hadn't made it home. It was still lying in the ditch beside the lane. With my luck it would probably rain all over the Prince of Denmark. . . .

I was just starting back toward the house with an armful of books when Red walked in through the gateway. "Sure takes you a long time to get from the bus to the house, don't it?" he said, giving my books a puzzled look.

"Yeah, well I got kind of distracted." I didn't go into detail. When Red ran into Kat he'd understand what distracted was all about.

I spotted Dad and Uncle Joe standing by the corral, looking at the imported Simmental bull that Frank Gillette, Dad's boss, had just bought. I set my books by the corner of the garage—they were getting closer to home all the time—and started toward the corral. "Come on, Red," I said, "I want you to meet my uncle."

Red didn't answer, and I turned to see if he'd heard me. He hadn't, mainly because he wasn't listening. He wasn't even looking in my direction. I followed his gaze; then I understood. Red had discovered Kat. She was sitting on the front porch, holding Tomte and having a big discussion with him. He was probably telling her how much he hated cold beans. It kind of surprised me that Tomte was letting her hold him at all. He usually has pretty good taste in people, and if a stranger tries getting too friendly too fast, he's likely to let them have it with a mean left hook. Somehow, though, Kat had him convinced that she was okay.

"Lance." Red's hushed voice interrupted my thoughts. "Who *is* that?"

"Kat," I said tiredly, knowing things were going to get more complicated than I wanted.

"I know the cat, dipstick. I mean the girl."

"That *is* the girl. Kat. K-A-T Ducharme. My cousin."

"Your cousin?" Red echoed, like he'd never heard the word. Either he was going deaf or his elevator wasn't going all the way to the top these days.

"Yeah, Paleface, that's what I said. The one I told you about on the phone about ten minutes ago. Remember?"

"She's a girl?" he said, still in that strange tone of voice. I wasn't sure if he was asking me or telling me, but either way I thought the fact was fairly obvious.

"Hey, come on, man," I said, starting to get irritated. "Haul your eyeballs back in their sockets, and let's go. She isn't all that interesting."

Finally, Red managed to unglue his eyes from her long enough to spare me a pitying look. "Geronimo," he said softly, "are you blind, or what? She's beautiful."

I looked at Red. He looked like he was coming down with something. I sighed—and took a long look at her myself. And for the first time since I'd dragged her off my horse, I had to admit that maybe it was true. Kat *was* kind of beautiful.

"Yeah," I said slowly, "you could be right about that. But," I added, "a Siberian tiger's beautiful too. And there's no way I'd turn my back on either one of them."

7

Well, I guess I should have seen it coming. Red and Kat, I mean. As long as I've known Red, he's always been like that. Show him a cute girl, and his brains turn to jelly. In fact, that's how we got to be friends in the first place—when I dragged him out of a fight he was having with some guy twice his size over some little twelve- going on twenty-nine-year-old-seventh-grade chick, who probably didn't like either one of them. I figured he might have learned something from that experience, but from that sick-calf look in his eyes right now, I could see I was wrong.

Personally, I'm not all that interested in girls. Don't get that wrong—I *like* girls just fine. I can pick a "10" out of a crowd with no trouble at all and I even let Bobbi-Jo Carson sit by me at the movies once in a while. What I mean is, I'm not about to get serious with a girl for a real long time. All this young love stuff might be okay for Romeo and Juliet—not that it worked out so great for them, when you stop to think about it—but I've lived the real side of it. My mom was only sixteen when she married my dad, seventeen when I was born—and twenty-two when she decided she was tired of being grown up and having a family, and took off to live the life she missed when she was a teenager.

Red and I walked on up to the porch. "Kat," I said, keeping it short and to the point, "this is Red." That sounded a little too short, so I added, "He's a friend of mine," which sounded stupid and unnecessary.

I didn't go through the motions of introducing Kat to Red. He already knew her name and didn't seem to need reminding. He had this stupid, puppy-dog grin all over his face, and all those manners his dad is always trying to drill into him had suddenly surfaced. For a second there, I was afraid he was going to bow, or kiss her hand, or start quoting *Romeo and Juliet*. But he pulled himself together. "Hi, Kat," he said, all cool like he knew what he was doing. "It's real nice to meet you at last."

At last? He'd known she existed for all of three minutes. I gave him a look, but he totally missed it. He was too busy staring into Kat's eyes like an optometrist about to make a diagnosis.

She looked back at him and smiled. Not her sassy smile, either. "I'm glad to meet you too, Red—" she said—I couldn't believe this was the same little shameless horse thief who'd almost ridden me into the dust. But Kat shot a sudden glance in my direction and renewed my faith in her "—even if you are a friend of Lance's," she added, talking to Red, but meaning it for me.

Right about then, Dad and Uncle Joe strolled over to the house, and I grabbed the chance to drag Red back to full consciousness and introduce him to Uncle Joe. Joe gave him the once-over, and I could see that Red had passed. I knew he would. Uncle Joe's a pretty good judge of people. I wasn't sure what Red thought of him but when they shook hands, Red was definitely impressed. Shaking hands with Uncle Joe is like hand-to-hand combat with a gravel crusher —only the strong survive.

While Red was recovering, I turned to Dad. "We're gonna run some salt up to the cows now, okay?"

Dad nodded. "Good idea. They'll be gettin' restless if they don't have any for more than a couple of days."

I started toward our old Dodge half-ton, but then the idea hit me. "Uh, Dad? You think maybe we could take the

Chev?" I said, real cool and laid back as if I drove it every day.

The Chev was brand-new—a three-quarter-ton four by four—and even though Dad's boss had bought it as a farm truck, he'd gone first class, as usual. It was loaded: carpet, air-conditioning, tape deck, power windows—you name it. In fact, Dad had been kind of disgusted when Frank turned up with a truck like that for him to use around the ranch doing chores. To Dad's way of thinking, it was a lot more comfortable to drive something that was already scratched up a little bit. But to my way of thinking, driving that Chev was the kind of discomfort I could take a lot of.

I've been driving for a long time. When you live on a ranch you learn young so you can help out running errands. I can even remember steering when I was still too short to reach the pedals. Dad would put the truck in low gear and set a rock on the gas pedal so the truck was barely moving. Then he'd jump out and climb into the back to throw off bales or something, and I'd just keep us from hitting any trees. From there on, Dad let me drive more and more until I got to drive all the time—around the ranch or on the back roads where he was pretty sure I wouldn't get caught. I won't be sixteen for another five months.

Dad looked first at me, then at the Chev. Then he looked back at me. "Might as well," he said, at last. "Frank bought it for doin' chores. Drive careful, hey." He always threw that in when I was driving somewhere—but it was what he said to his friends when they drove off too. It was just his way of saying good-bye; he didn't mean it as a warning.

"You got it, Dad." I grinned at him over my shoulder.

"Come on, Red," I said, nudging him in the ribs to get his attention. "Let's load up that salt." Reluctantly, he followed me to the truck. I had a feeling he might like Kat even better than he liked the Chev.

I threw the last block of salt into the truck and opened the door to get in, but Red stopped me. "Aren't you gonna ask Kat to come along?" he demanded in a low voice.

I shrugged. "Hadn't figured on it," I muttered, but even as I said it, I knew I'd never get away with it. Not unless I wanted to get rid of one red-headed friend real fast. Anyhow, I figured Dad might have a few ideas on the subject of being polite to company.

I met Red's accusing look. "Okay, okay, don't get your freckles on fire. You want her to come, *you* ask her."

I got in and sat there just breathing in that new smell and pretending it was my truck. Just thinking it made me feel about five years older and a whole lot richer. It even mellowed my mood enough for me to forgive Red when he gallantly opened the door for Kat and settled her between us on the seat.

I turned the key with my left hand and shuddered as the sound of Willie Nelson filled the cab. Dad and I had been hauling bales yesterday and flipped to see who'd pick the music. He'd won. I yanked out the tape and stuck in another that was lying on the dash. The driving beat of my old "Born in the USA" tape blasted out of the speakers. That was better.

Kat gave me a dirty look. "I *like* Willie," she said.

I grinned and turned Bruce up a little louder.

I thought about spinning a little gravel as I took off, but with Dad and Uncle Joe leaning on the fence watching, I thought again. But I drove fast—as usual. With power steering and an automatic transmission, driving mostly one-handed was pretty easy. And my right hand was good enough to keep the wheel steady if I wanted to open a window or something. I took one or two glances at Red and Kat, but watching them smile at each other like they were making a toothpaste commercial was more than I could stand, so I concentrated on the trail ahead.

Suddenly I yanked the wheel hard to the right, so hard I instinctively tried to close my right hand around it and got a jolt of pain all the way to the elbow for my trouble. But I missed the rock. I should have remembered that rock; I'd been driving around it for years. But the grass was extra tall this year.

I glanced over at Red and Kat. They were both staring at me like I'd lost my mind. "Show-off," Kat muttered under her breath. Typical, I thought. She didn't even see the rock, missed the whole point of that fancy bit of steering, and managed to come out blaming me for something—what, she wasn't sure. I ignored her and kept my mind on watching out for more rocks. But when I hit the brakes a couple of minutes later, it wasn't because of a rock.

It was something just as bad, though. An old, dead poplar tree had fallen down in the last big wind, breaking the three-wire fence between us and the neighbor's place. Fifty-some head of cows had discovered the hole. Right now those cows were heading for the neighbor's crop of ripe oats like somebody'd just hollered Dinner! That spelled trouble.

The fast stop jolted Red back to reality. "Oh, great," he groaned, opening his door and jumping out before I had even stopped the truck. I was out half a second after him. "I'll get around the leaders!" he yelled as he started to sprint in a big circle to head off the cows before they could get to the oats.

"Okay, I'll turn the rest back down along the fence," I answered, starting to run too.

"Hey!" Kat's voice stopped me. "What about me?"

"Can you drive that thing?" I asked.

She tossed her head like a bad-mannered horse. "What do you think?" she demanded. She wouldn't have given me a straight answer if I'd asked which way was up.

"Then turn it around, and go back to that gate in the corner we passed about a mile back and open it. Then get out of the way. We'll chase the cows out through there. And hurry up!"

I didn't wait for an answer. As I took off in hot pursuit of the last few cows, I saw Kat slide behind the wheel and put the truck into a tight turn. It looked like she knew what she was doing, so I concentrated on the cows. Way up ahead, Red was involved in a match race with a rangy old long-horned Hereford who wasn't about to give up dinner without a struggle. My money was on Red, though. He'd really got into long-distance running lately, and I figured he'd been training harder than that cow had—which reminded me that I was planning to watch him run in the county cross-country race tomorrow.

But that was tomorrow. This was now, and I was losing ground on a pair of half-grown calves, who seemed to be enjoying this sport a whole lot more than I was. It crossed my mind that if God had meant people to run races with cows, he never would have made horses. Puffing and sweating, I finally managed to come up alongside the calves. "Heeyah!" I screeched at them, hoping I sounded as fierce as one of my long-lost ancestors on the warpath. I'd have made a great warrior—especially if I'd have been fighting baby cows. These two did a double take, gave me an astonished look through their long, innocent white eyelashes, and headed back for their mothers as fast as they could go.

Red had outlasted the Hereford. She turned away from the oatfield and was leading the bunch down the fence line at a gallop. Now if Kat just got that gate open in time . . . I caught a flash of chrome as the truck disappeared over a hill ahead of the cows. She wasn't wasting any time.

The gate was open—and Kat was standing in exactly the right place to make sure they turned and went out through it. They did—and like a bunch of bad kids who know they're in big trouble, they just kept on going till they were out of sight. They'd stay away long enough for us to go home and pick up some tools to fix the fence. The salt would have to wait.

The three of us headed for the truck. Red took a look at

me and grinned. "You ain't gettin' any faster, Geronimo," he said, breathing disgustingly easy for somebody who'd just run that far.

"Yeah?" I retaliated, puffing like a wind-broken horse. "Well, just 'cause you're built like an undernourished greyhound . . ."

Kat turned around and looked us both over. "I was hopin' for the long-horned cow," she said, straight-faced. "She had more style than the two of you put together." Then she flashed a wicked smile over her shoulder. "First one to the truck gets to drive home," she challenged, already breaking into a run as she said it.

Well, in the first place, she was already about ten yards ahead of us; in the second place, she hadn't just finished competing in the Hereford Olympics like we had; and, in the third place, she could run like the wind. Even Red didn't come close to catching her.

She slid behind the wheel, turned the key and then just sat there, daring me to do anything about it. I knew getting her out of the driver's seat would be harder than getting her off my horse had been, so I didn't try. I climbed in next to her—partly to keep an eye on her driving, but mostly to make Red mad. Since he didn't have much choice, Red got in next to me.

I looked at Kat. "Well," I said, "what you waitin' for? If you're drivin', drive." She pulled Bruce out of the tape deck, put Willie back in, turned him up real loud, and drove.

8

I should have noticed the noise in the motor a lot sooner than I did. But with old Willie wailing and the rest of us talking and laughing, it was pretty hard to hear anything in there. Yeah, I was making my share of the noise. Somehow the great cow chase had lightened things up some between me and Kat and, much as I hated to admit it, I was almost starting to enjoy myself.

But that sound finally registered in my brain, sending shivers up the back of my neck. Because a brand new engine doesn't start knocking like that unless there's something real serious wrong with it.

"Hey, what's that?" I said, suddenly reaching for the volume control and cutting Willie off in mid-bleat.

"What's what?" Red asked, and Kat gave me a startled look.

"That," I said, but I didn't need to. In the sudden silence of the cab, you could hear that motor hammering away like there was a carpenters' convention going on under the hood.

"Slow down," I ordered as I leaned over to check the dials on the instrument panel. And there it was, burning like a single, evil red eye, the oil pressure warning light. My stomach gave a lurch. "Kat," I said, managing to keep my voice calm, "how long has that light been on?"

"What li . . ." she began, but then she flashed a glance at the instrument panel and the question stopped right there. I'd got my answer, though. She didn't have a clue, I thought disgustedly. I should have known better than to let her drive.

"Stop the truck," I said.

Kat hesitated. "Lance, what's wrong with—" she began.

I didn't give her time to finish. Something was wrong here and, if it was what I was afraid it was, every second that motor kept running was making it worse. "I said 'Stop'!" I snapped at her.

All of a sudden the engine missed, missed again, sputtered, and died. We jerked to a standstill.

We all looked at each other, but nobody said anything. Then Red had his door open and was jumping out, with me right behind him. Over my shoulder, I could see Kat climbing out of the driver's side.

We all walked around the back. And what we saw proved that I'd guessed right—though being right had never felt worse.

A wounded animal will keep running as long as it can, leaving a trail of blood behind it. And a wounded machine isn't much different. It just bleeds a different color. Black. Oil. From the looks of the long, black line that marked our back trail as far as I could see, I figured that truck had lost an awful lot of it. Maybe enough to be fatal.

Red was bending down underneath. Now he looked up and said what I was already thinking. "Oil pan's ripped wide open," he said, sounding like the voice of doom. I nodded silently. I didn't want to see it for myself. But there was something I had to try, even though I knew it wasn't going to do any good. I walked around, got in behind the wheel, and turned the key. Nothing. It wouldn't even turn over. Red and Kat had followed me, and when I got out again Red gave me a questioning look. I shook my head and walked slowly around to the front of the truck, trying to think.

I couldn't believe this was really happening. It was all so

stupid. I mean, if she'd rolled it or smashed it into a tree, it would have been bad enough, but at least I could have understood how it could happen. But to hit something that hard and never say a word about it, and then just keep on driving, warning light and all, till the engine seized up . . .

I reached inside the grille for the hood release lever. Looking under the hood wasn't going to tell me anything I didn't already know, but it was something to do. And I'd do anything to put off telling Dad what we'd done to Frank's truck.

Then I realized I couldn't even open the hood. It was one of those complicated safety latches that takes two hands to release. There were two people with two good hands each standing within six feet of me, but I was determined to do this by myself or not at all. It turned out to be not at all. I kept trying till I skinned all my knuckles and tore off a fingernail so low it bled. I jerked my hand out, said a few choice words, and hauled off and kicked the bumper.

Red gave me a strange look. "Hey, come on, Geronimo, cool it, huh? I'll get that for you." He stepped up and opened the hood, dead easy, like it was for any normal person.

And then I was mad at him too. "Forget it, Red," I burst out. "Lookin' in there isn't gonna help. The motor's ratched. . . ."

Red gave me another look, but he didn't say anything. He just closed the hood.

I spun around and started walking toward the house. I might as well get this over with. But before I could take two steps, Kat stopped me. "Lance?"

"What?" I said, my voice cold.

"Don't you even want to hear what happened?" she asked, so quiet it didn't even sound like her.

"I know what happened. You weren't watchin' where you were goin' when you were alone back there, and you hit something; and instead of having sense enough to stop and check the damage, you just kept drivin' along, happy as could be, until all the oil ran out and the engine seized up. How's that? Pretty close?" I asked sarcastically.

Kat swallowed, but her voice was steady when she answered. "Yeah," she said, with just a trace of the usual defiance in those storm-cloud eyes. "That's pretty close. But I *did* stop. I felt this big bump and heard a scraping sound, and I stopped right away. I guess it was a rock under there, but I didn't see it in time. The grass was so tall. . . ."

My conscience gave a weak little flutter. I had come *so* close to hitting that same rock.

Kat went on, "I was gonna get out and look. I even had the door open, and then I saw how far ahead the cows were; and I knew if I waited, they were gonna get to the gate before I did. . . ." She stopped and looked at me, waiting. Waiting for what? For me to say it wasn't her fault?

"And you didn't think it was worth mentioning afterward, huh?" I said.

Kat's gaze dropped to the ground. She reached down and picked a stalk of ripe timothy. "I forgot about it," she said softly.

Just like that. She forgot about it, and that's supposed to excuse burning the motor out of a fifteen-thousand-dollar truck.

"Yeah." All the stored-up bitterness of one of the lousiest days of my life went into that word. I turned away again. But she still didn't get the message. "Lance . . ."

I swung around to face her again. I think if she'd have been a guy, I would have slugged her right then.

I took a deep breath. "What?" I said through my teeth.

"What are we gonna do about the truck?"

It was the wrong question, especially since I'd been asking myself the same thing for the past ten minutes and not getting any right answers. "What do you mean *we*?" I exploded. "*You* got nothin' to worry about. *I'm* the one Dad trusted with the truck. *I'm* the one who should've known better than to turn it over to some empty-headed little girl who can't even ride a horse, let alone drive a truck, without showin' off and wreckin' something. So I'll tell you what *I'm* gonna do. *I'm* gonna go and try to explain to Dad how his boss's new truck happens to need a new motor. All *you* have to do is nothin'. You've already done enough."

I ran out of breath then, but it didn't make any difference. I'd said it all. And Kat had just stood there and took it. For the first time I could remember, she didn't even fight back, and that left me feeling kind of guilty. For a second, I wondered if she was going to start crying. As far as I knew, I'd never made a girl cry before, and I didn't really want to break that record now.

But then this was Kat. And nobody made her cry. . . . She just held her head a little higher and looked at me. It was a look I didn't want to meet right then. I walked away. This time she didn't follow.

Red had been close enough to hear that whole conversation but he'd stayed out of it—a fact which I appreciated— until now. "Hey, man," he said, coming up behind me and grabbing my arm, "what's the matter with you, anyway?" His voice was low but hard-edged. "Don't you think she feels bad enough already? You didn't have to be so hard on her. She didn't mean to do it."

I jerked loose from him. "So she didn't mean to. Big deal. Most people who drive their cars over other people don't mean to. But they still go to jail. She should've known better."

"Oh, come on, Lance. How could she know better than to hit a rock she couldn't even see?"

"Well, maybe she couldn't help hittin' it, but she could've said something about it. That doesn't take much of an IQ."

"Well, you sure can't blame her for not tellin' *you*. The way you've been reacting to things lately, she was probably scared to . . ."

"Get serious, Red. She's never been scared of anything

46

in her life—me included. Stop makin' excuses for her just because you think she's 'beautiful' "—I gift wrapped that word in sarcasm. "I wouldn't have done anything that stupid, and neither would you."

"Oh, yeah?" he shot back at me. He was trying to yell quietly, and I could see it wasn't easy. "Who are you tryin' to kid? You want a list of a few of the dumb things you've done, give me a day or two. And, besides, what you keep forgettin'—how, I'll never know—is that she's a *girl*. How can you expect her to know all about motors and stuff? Give her a break."

I groaned. Now, on top of everything else, he'd gone gallant on me again. "Oh, yeah, for sure, Red. She's just a poor, helpless, delicate little girl. Well, why don't you try tellin' that to her. You might look better with your face rearranged. I've tried treatin' her like a girl and, believe me, it don't work. I'm not about to start tryin' it again now."

Red blew out his breath in a long sigh that made me think of an old locomotive letting off steam before it blew its boiler completely. "Geronimo," he muttered, "you have got to be the most . . ." He ran out of words and threw his hands up in a helpless gesture.

I sighed too. Whatever he'd been going to say, I figured he was probably right.

9

It was less than a quarter of a mile from where the truck stopped to the house, but it was the longest walk of my life. Red was right. I had done some pretty dumb things in my day—but not many of them had involved disappointing my dad. When you grow up with one parent being both mom and dad there's no middle ground in the way you feel about them. You either end up hating them or loving them twice as much. And I loved Dad.

Our relationship wouldn't make sense to a lot of people. Dad isn't your typical parent. In fact, I can still remember a time when I had to sit there and listen while some social worker went on about how Dad lacked "parenting skills"— whatever they are. Maybe she meant that Dad didn't treat me like a kid. And she was right about that. He never did. From the time I was real small, it was more like we were partners, just him and me against the world. He'd show me the right way to do something, tell me why it was that way, and then, if I thought I could handle the job, he'd let me try it.

And he never nags me about the little stuff—haircuts and homework and all that junk that some parents—Red's, for instance—think is real earthshaking. Mostly, Dad just leaves that kind of thing up to me. I make my own choices, and I live with the results.

But the big things are different. That's when I pay my

dues in responsibility. And when I mess up, I answer to him.

Dad and Uncle Joe were sitting on the porch, drinking coffee and watching curiously as the three of us came straggling into the yard. As I came up to the porch Uncle Joe's voice boomed out. "Hey, Lance, didn't anybody ever tell you you gotta put gas in them things to make 'em go?" He laughed, but I couldn't even manage a grin.

I guess the look on my face must have spelled out real bad news because Uncle Joe's smile faded. He and Dad both sat there, not saying anything—waiting. I hesitated a minute at the bottom of the steps, thinking about how much easier it would be if I were dead and buried.

Then I did what I guess I'd known all along I'd have to do. For only the second time in my life that I could remember, I looked Dad right in the eye and I lied to him. It wasn't a total lie, but it was a long ways from the whole truth. It felt like a lie to me.

"Dad?" I said, surprised my voice sounded so calm. "I, uh, wrecked the truck."

There was a silence that felt like forever. A lot of things happened during that silence. I noticed that Kat and Red had come up and were standing there too. And when Kat heard what I said, her eyes suddenly widened. She started to take a step forward, and I knew that she was going to blow my story wide open if I didn't stop her. I blazed her a look that should have set her hair on fire. She'd got me into this mess. The least she could do was let me handle it my own way. It was pretty obvious she didn't think so, though. She looked about ready to blow a fuse. But for now she stood still and kept her mouth shut, and that was all I asked.

Dad looked at me. Then he looked at the truck, sitting over there at the edge of the field, its chrome winking mockingly in the setting sun. "You *what*?" he asked at last, his voice dangerously soft.

I swallowed. "I hit a rock, and it tore a hole in the oil pan, and, well, I never noticed we were losin' oil until the engine seized up. . . ."

I couldn't tell from Dad's face how mad he was; mostly he was still registering complete disbelief. I couldn't decide what it was that he didn't believe, my story or my stupidity. Or both. It didn't really matter, though. I just felt lousy—as much for the lie as for the truck. But not as lousy as I would have felt if I'd let Kat take the blame.

Slowly, without taking his eyes off my face, Dad stood up. "You didn't *notice.*" It was almost a whisper. And the quieter Dad gets, the closer he is to blowing up.

Just then, Uncle Joe decided to get involved in the whole mess. Maybe the timing was a coincidence, but I doubted it. The tension between me and Dad was thick enough to carve your initials in.

Uncle Joe stood up and casually laid a hand on Dad's shoulder. "Come on, Mike," he said, cool as ever. "Let's go check out the damage." Dad hesitated a few seconds, still looking at me in a way that almost made me wish he'd go ahead and hit me and get it over with. Then he sighed and turned to walk with Joe toward the truck. I followed, and Kat and Red tagged along behind me.

I stood back while Dad and Uncle Joe looked the truck over. Joe was the mechanic of the family—anybody who could keep *The Falcon* flying had to be a mechanic. They took in that long trail of oil like a pair of detectives studying a smoking gun. Then, despite the fact that he was wearing what looked like a brand-new, white cowboy shirt, Uncle Joe eased his bulk under the truck. He threshed around under there for a while, muttering to himself, came out looking like a grease monkey at the end of a long, hard day, and went to have a look under the hood. Dad stuck his head under there too, and I peered over their shoulders. I had a personal interest—kind of like the personal interest a condemned killer has in the way the electric chair works.

Joe stepped back, slammed the hood down, and wiped his hands on his pants. "Yup," he said. "She's had the biscuit, all right."

Dad sighed. "Whole new motor?" He asked. His fists were clenched so tight his knuckles were white.

" 'Fraid so. Might as well set this one in the front yard and plant petunias in it 'cause it sure ain't goin' any farther."

Dad shook his head. "How much you figure?"

Uncle Joe gazed thoughtfully at the truck. "One of these big, eight-cylinder jobs? Bad news, Mike. Eight, nine hundred. Maybe more, the way things keep goin' up."

My stomach lurched—and as Dad turned toward me, it lurched again. Okay, I thought. This is it.

But Dad didn't lay a hand on me. He didn't even look at me. He just walked right past me like I wasn't even there. He wasn't going to hit me, I thought, taking a deep breath. But I wasn't all that relieved. Because getting beat up was something I could handle. At least that kind of pain is quick and clean—like getting cut with a sharp knife. When Dad turned his back on me though, it meant I'd lost his trust—and that was a whole lot worse.

I stood there watching him walk away. He walked bent forward a little like he was fighting a strong wind—or carrying a heavy load. I knew, feeling kind of hollow inside, that on a ranch hand's wages, a thousand bucks had to go a long way. But I also knew that, however hard it would be, Dad would pay for that motor out of his own pocket because that's the way Dad is. He might be just a half-breed cowboy without much money or education, but he's got more pride and honor than most of the people who are running this country.

Sure, he could get away with slipping an extra-big repair bill into general expenses, and Frank wouldn't question it. He was hardly ever around anyway, and actually making money off the ranch was the least of his worries. But I knew

51

Dad wouldn't do it that way. Nothing but pure, unnecessary carelessness had wrecked that motor: I had been responsible for it and, the way Dad saw it, he was responsible for what I did.

The next thing I knew I was breaking into a run to catch up with him. "Dad?" No answer. He kept walking. "Dad," I said, my voice getting a little louder.

He stopped and turned impatiently. His face was as bleak as a blizzard in February. "What do you want?" he asked, his voice rough.

I hesitated. The words didn't come easy. "Dad," I swallowed. "I'm sorry . . ." I was going to say more, but I never got the chance.

"Well, sorry ain't always good enough," Dad cut in. "You better remember that next time you trade in your common sense and start showin' off to impress some girl."

Stunned, I stared at him. *That* was what he thought? That this whole thing had happened because I'd been showing off for Kat? That I could forget what he'd spent fifteen years teaching me about responsibility over *her*? That was crazy—wasn't it? Remembering the way I'd been acting ever since I found her out there on my horse, I could see where he'd got that idea—even though he was dead wrong.

I didn't even try to argue with him about it. The mood he was in, I knew it was no use. But I did try something else. "I've got a couple hundred dollars saved up . . ." I began.

But he didn't let me finish that sentence either. "You think that's what this is all about," he said. "The money?"

I shook my head. "No," I said, miserably, "I know it's not about the money." But I felt like adding, What *is* it about, then, Dad? You don't want my apology. You don't want my money. What else *do* you want from me?

Maybe the look on my face said some of what I was thinking because Dad's face softened a little. "First thing in the morning we'll haul the truck into the machine shed and pull that motor. You can start by helping with that."

"Okay," I said. And then I remembered what had caused this whole thing in the first place. "There's a hole in the fence between us and Glover's about three miles up there. You want me to go fix it?" I asked.

Dad shook his head. "No, I'll take care of it." That's all he said, but I knew he was thinking, You've done enough damage for one day.

We'd walked back to the yard by now. Dad threw some tools in the Dodge and hollered at Uncle Joe, who was over by the corral talking to the bull and staying out of the family fight. Joe got in, and they drove off.

I watched as they detoured around the Chev and disappeared into the deepening shadows of the woods. Then Red and Kat came walking into the yard. Red said something and started walking in my direction. Kat shook her black mane and headed for the house, tossing a furious look over her shoulder—and almost tripping on the bottom step as she did. It was the best thing that had happened all day.

Red came over and leaned on the fence beside me. "So," he said, "you get it sorted out with your dad?"

"No."

"He was pretty mad, huh?"

"No madder than he had a right to be," I said.

Red nodded. "Yeah," he said. "For a minute there, I wasn't so sure how he was going to react." Generally, Red gets along better with my dad than he does with his own, but he's also seen enough of the results of Dad's fast and physical discipline to have a healthy respect for his temper.

"Me neither," I said. "But he never laid a hand on me." Then I added something that almost surprised me. "You know, I kinda wish he had."

Red nodded. "Yeah, I know what you mean." As far as I knew, Red's dad had never hit him. He just laid guilt on him instead. And as I was beginning to find out, that's not necessarily the easy way out.

Red looked at his watch. "Hey," he said, "I'd better get goin'. I promised Dad I'd be home early and get lots of sleep for tomorrow. He's had me in training for that cross-country like it's the Olympics." He said it kind of embarrassed—but kind of proud too. For his dad and him to be able to do anything together without getting into a major war was quite an accomplishment. Now it seemed strange how things were kind of reversed. Red and his dad were getting along good—and Dad and I were barely talking to each other.

"Guess I won't be goin' to see you run after all," I said, automatically falling in beside him as he started down the lane.

He looked at me. "Your dad *grounded* you?" He knew grounding wasn't Dad's style.

"Not exactly. He didn't say anything, but I think I'm grounded anyway. That make sense?"

Red grinned. "About as much sense as you ever do, Geronimo."

We'd come to the end of the lane. "Give me a call when you get home tomorrow, okay?" I said.

"For sure. If it's not too late, maybe I'll come over and see how you're doin'." Translated, I figured that meant how Kat was doin', but I let him get away with it. I was too tired for another argument.

Red started down the road. "Hey, Paleface!" I called after him. He stopped. "Run good tomorrow, huh?"

10

I didn't feel like going back to the house, so I climbed through the fence and took a long, slow tour of the horse pasture. I wandered around talking to all the horses, even Spider who came up and nibbled the back of my neck and apologized for forgetting whose horse he was this afternoon. I hung out there until it was pitch-dark, but when I stepped in a badger hole and nearly broke my leg, I gave up and headed for the house.

I couldn't see any lights. Maybe everybody had gone to bed, which was fine with me. That was all I wanted to do right now too. I was halfway up the porch steps when, right beside me, something moved. I jumped about two feet straight sideways and was already feeling foolish by the time I landed.

It was just Uncle Joe sitting there all by himself with his feet up on the veranda railing, watching a huge, orange moon edge its way over the treetops. "Spook you?" he asked.

I shrugged. "Yeah, sort of. I thought everybody'd gone to bed."

"Your dad has. Kat's in there watchin' TV. One of them sad love stories women like to cry their eyes out over."

"Bet Kat ain't cryin' her eyes out."

Joe chuckled at that, but then he added, "You might be surprised."

Before I had time to wonder about that, he reached out

and pulled over another chair. "Sit down and help me make sure that moon don't get caught in the top of that big old poplar there on the hill," he said. I sat down. I hadn't thought I felt like company—but Uncle Joe was special.

Sometimes it was hard for me to believe that Dad and him were brothers; they were so different. I guess if I compared them to horses, Dad would be the plow horse—strong, honest, and reliable, staying in his rut and doing a good, steady job. But Uncle Joe was a thoroughbred, hot-blooded and crazy, too unpredictable to be much good around the farm—but lightning in the backstretch. The two of them lived in two different worlds—even, as far as I could tell, when they were growing up in the same house.

Dad had quit school young, I knew that; but even though he'd never actually said so, I was pretty sure he had to quit to work and help support the family. Uncle Joe had quit too, but he'd done it to play hockey. He'd been the local star in town, and Dad had told me he'd got as far as playing semipro somewhere—Edmonton, I think. According to Dad, Joe had been good enough to have a pretty fair chance of making the big leagues. Except that after about a year he got sick of living in the city, dropped the whole idea, and got a job with a guide and outfitter up in the Yukon somewhere. Then, after a year, some rich American rancher up there on a hunting trip decided he liked Uncle Joe's style and offered him a job on his place in Texas.

Well, after that Dad lost track of him for a couple of years—that was back in the sixties—and, the next thing Dad heard, Joe was flying helicopters in Vietnam. How he ended up there, nobody knows. Maybe he took out American citizenship and got drafted, but then again it would have been like him to volunteer just to find out what was going on. I guess he found out, all right. I tried asking him about what it was like, but mostly he wouldn't talk about it. Except the flying. He loved that so much that a few years later he was back in Canada with enough money saved up to buy his own plane and a half interest in a guide and outfitting business at Fort St. John.

I guess he was finally ready to settle down because he's been there about twelve years now. Of course, marrying Kat's mom helped settle him down too. Dad says that Aunt Jean is the best thing that ever happened to Joe, and he's probably right. She's quite a lady—the kind who can throw a diamond hitch on a dozen packhorses and a turkey dinner for thirty people equally easy. And on the same day too. She takes everything in her stride, including Uncle Joe.

Uncle Joe pulled out a pack of cigarettes, took one, then held them out to me. "This one of your vices?" he asked.

I shook my head. "No thanks, I quit."

"Smart kid. Guess I'm gonna have to kick the habit one of these days with Kat and her mom both terrorizing me so bad at home that I've got in the habit of sneakin' one outside after dark. Don't know why I'm doin' it here. Guess I'm still halfways expectin' Mike to get on my case if I don't behave."

"Dad?" I said, not sure I'd heard right. The last thing I could picture was Dad intimidating Uncle Joe.

Joe laughed. "Yeah," he said, "old habits die slow. Mike may be only two years older than me, but in a lot of ways he practically raised me. Seemed like whenever I got in trouble—which was fair regular—he was there, either bailin' me out or givin' me heck. Usually both."

"Yeah?" I said, real interested. Dad never talked much about when he was a kid. "Where was your dad?" I asked. "How come he didn't do that stuff?"

Joe studied the glowing end of his cigarette for a minute. "Our old man," he said at last, like he was stating a fact, not giving an opinion, "wasn't much good."

I waited and he went on. "He never could hold onto a steady job. He drank. And when he drank, he was mean as sin and lookin' for somebody to beat up. Mom. Us kids. All of us sometimes. Mom spent half her life tiptoein' around, tryin' not to do anything to rile him when he'd been drinkin', and Mike usually had sense enough to lie low when Pop was on the rampage. 'Course, I didn't have any more sense about that than I did about anything else; and I was always pullin' some fool stunt when he was feelin' mean, and almost gettin' my head took off—when he didn't take it out on Mike instead, that is."

Joe took a deep drag on his cigarette and rocked back in his chair. "Yeah," he said, "poor old Mike was always catchin' it for stuff I'd done. I remember once when I was about twelve I took Pop's brand-new fishin' rod—fishin' was about as close to useful work as the old man came— and, of course, I managed to bust it.

"Well, when Pop found out it was wrecked, there was hell to pay. For some reason it was Mike he tackled. He went plumb crazy and started yellin' and knockin' him around. And I was sittin' there all the time, right in the same room. One word from Mike, and it would have been me that got it. But Mike didn't say anything." The moon had made it over the poplar tree, and the light hit Uncle Joe's face as he turned to me. "Pop beat Mike black-and-blue over that stupid fishin' rod," he said slowly, "but he never once let on it was me that wrecked it. And you know, Lance," he said, giving me a look that was hard to read, "to this day, I can't decide if that made him a hero or a fool. . . ." Then he switched on a big alligator-grin and, although moonlight is tricky stuff, I could have sworn I saw him wink. "But I sure did admire his guts . . ."

Now why had he picked that particular bedtime story? I wondered nervously. Did he know something I didn't think he knew? I tried to think of a fast way to change the subject.

But then Uncle Joe kind of changed it himself. "Yeah," he said, "that's the way it always was. Still is. I got us into trouble, and Mike got us out. I think he must have been born grown up. I go blastin' into things like a runaway Brahma and never know where I've landed till the dust clears, while Mike just keeps both feet on the ground and makes sure he don't make stupid mistakes."

It was getting late, and I'd half put myself to sleep staring at the moon and listening to Uncle Joe's deep, gentle voice. "He made one mistake," I said, hardly realizing I'd said it, not just thought it. "He married my mom." And right away, I wished I could take the words back. I think about my mom all the time, but I don't talk about her.

Uncle Joe gave me a strange look. And when he started talking again his voice was thoughtful. "I dunno," he said, "Wasn't it Shakespeare or one of them old English poets that said it was better to have loved and lost than never to have loved at all? And"—he was dead serious now—"Mike sure did love that woman."

I sat there frozen by the spell of the moonlight and those words. I wanted him to go on—and yet I didn't. But then Uncle Joe lightened up again. "Anyhow," he said, "your dad didn't lose everything. He got you, didn't he?"

That broke the spell. I gave him a sheepish grin. "Yeah," I said, wearily, "but if you asked him right now, I don't think Dad would figure that was exactly hittin' the jackpot."

Joe laughed and reached over a big paw to mess up my hair. "Don't take it so hard about the truck, kid. Mike ain't as mad as he's makin' out. He just expects an awful lot of you. Besides, he works too hard and takes life too serious. I tried to tell him that. I might have known I'd never talk him into comin'."

"Comin' where?" I asked.

"Didn't I get around to tellin' you what I came down here for in the first place?" He didn't wait for an answer. "Well, I figured your dad could use a holiday, and"—he paused—"I also figured I could use the best horse handler in Alberta to help me with a little project I've got goin'."

"Yeah?" I said, starting to get real interested.

Uncle Joe ground out his cigarette and sat up a little straighter. "Me and my partner just bought ourselves a new huntin' territory. Country so wild it practically growls at you," he explained, getting a dreamy look in his eyes. "But there's one little catch—it's eighty miles cross-country from where I've got my base camp now. And, somehow, I've gotta trail twenty-five head of saddle- and packhorses over there. So I came down to see if Mike—and you, too, if they'd parole you from school for a week—wanted to come along for a little trail ride."

Did I want to go? Did tigers have stripes?

But then reality hit. "And Dad said no?" I asked, unbelievingly.

Uncle Joe nodded. "That's what he said, all right. He told me about bales to stack, and oats to cut, and cows to sort, and fences to fix until I ached all over just thinkin' about that much work."

I was too disappointed to say anything, but as I pushed back my chair and slowly stood up, Uncle Joe read my mind. "Hey, come on, cowboy. Don't take it so hard," he said with a big smile. "You can still come, even if he don't . . ."

For a minute my spirits started to rise, but then they hit a big downdraft. I shook my head. "Try tellin' that to Dad," I said tiredly. "The mood he's in, I ain't goin' nowhere." I had a feeling that for the next while my spare time was already planned—stacking bales, cutting oats, sorting cows.

11

I walked into the dark living room—and almost stepped on Kat. She was lying on the floor, munching on a humongous sandwich and so absorbed in some tear-jerking love scene that she never even looked up. That was fine with me. But looking at her sandwich had made me hungry. I started toward the kitchen to make my own, but I didn't get there. Suddenly Kat sat up. "So, Lancelot," she said sarcastically, "you feel like a hero now?"

I stopped in my tracks. This time she really had flipped out. "What?" I said, not even sure I'd heard her right.

"Oh, don't be so modest about it. Don't you usually rescue at least one damsel in distress every day?"

I walked back over to her. "You are makin' exactly zero sense, Kat. I don't know what you're on, but . . ."

And that really set her off. She came to her feet like a leopard. For the first time, I noticed that I was two or three inches taller than her now. At least that was an improvement. But anything that Kat lacked in height, she made up for in temper. She was spitting fire. "What *I'm* on? That's good, comin' from Alderton's very own teenage drug dealer. . . ."

"Aw, come on, Kat. It wasn't like that . . ." I began, but she wasn't listening.

"You really are full of surprises, aren't you? From druggie to knight in shining armor without even using a phone booth."

I'd had enough. "Kat!" I yelled. "If for once in your life you'd shut up long enough for—"

"Long enough for you to tell some more lies? Is that it, Lance? Shut up and let you do things the way you want, and never mind what anybody else might want? Who gave you the right to lie for me, anyway? You were so busy playin' hero that you never once stopped to think about how I might feel. Well, I'll tell you how I feel. Lousy, that's how. What do you think—I don't have guts enough to take the blame for my own mistakes? It was me who drove over that rock, and I feel bad enough about that. But I sure don't need you to make it worse by sayin' you did it."

There must have been at least five questions in that speech, I decided; but never once had she stopped long enough to let me answer even one. "Kat, what is it with you, anyhow?" I cut in at last, wondering if it would help any to bang my head against the wall. "You're mad at me most of the time because I'm not nice to you. Okay, even I can follow that. So I try bein' nice. And then you're really mad. And that I'm havin' a little trouble followin'. Is there anything in this whole, entire world I could do that wouldn't make you mad?"

"Yeah," she shot back instantly, "you could quit actin' like . . ." Her voice trailed off and I waited. I really did want to know what she thought I was acting like. But she didn't finish. "Oh, forget it," she said, tossing her hair back. "Just leave me alone. Go away. A long way away."

I almost asked her where she thought I should go, seeing as how I lived here, and all. But just then the credits rolled across the TV screen. "And now you've even made me miss the end of the movie," she said, giving me a nasty glare. She stood up and turned the TV off with a slap that made me wonder what it had done to offend her. Then she stalked off up the stairs like she was the Queen of England.

Suddenly, I realized how tired I was. I didn't bother with the sandwich after all. Somehow, in the last five minutes,

I'd lost my appetite. I was sick and tired of World War III, just Kat and me.

If I could only get her to listen for about five minutes . . . Slowly I headed upstairs for my room.

Then a familiar sound stopped me. Ker-thump. Ker-thump. The sound of an overweight, three-legged cat climbing the stairs. On nights when he doesn't have anything better lined up, Tomte sleeps in my room. This must be one of those nights. I stood there, patiently waiting for him.

He reached the top of the stairs, paused, and took a careful look around—checking for stray saber-toothed tigers, I supposed. Then he sat down, licked his paw, and gave his face a swipe or two. I sighed. Tomte does not hurry.

"Here, Tom. Come on, fella," I called softly, hoping that Kat didn't choose this moment to stick her head out her door. I don't know what's so embarrassing about getting caught calling your cat, but right then it seemed real uncool.

"Mrrup," Tomte said and stood up. Slowly he came over to my door, sat down in front of me, and gave my ankle two thorough whisker rubs. Then he just sat there, purring like a Boeing 747 revving its motors. "Okay, okay, I know you love me. Skip the serenade. I'm goin' to bed. If you're sleepin' with me, you better get in here." Tomte looked up, smiled a cat smile, and took one step into the room. Just then, there was a noise in the room across the hall. It sounded like Kat had opened the window. Tomte heard it too. He cocked his ears in that direction, fascinated by the idea that someone was in that usually empty room. He turned and, with great dignity, limped back out into the hall, sat down in front of Kat's door and, very delicately, began to pat the corner of it with his paw.

"Hey! What do you think you're doin'?" I heard Kat yell. From her tone, I knew she thought it was me out there. I heard her footsteps coming toward the door. Well, now was my chance to talk to her . . .

But, at the last second, I chickened out and silently pulled my door shut. Her door opened. "What do you—" I heard her begin—and then her voice changed. "Well, hello, baby. Did you come to see me?" she said in a tone reserved for animals and people she didn't hate—Red, for instance. "Well, come on in, beautiful."

"Mrrup," said the cat. Kat's door closed, and there were no more cat sounds in the hall. Obviously Tomte had made his choice. Disgusted, I went to bed. Alone.

I reached over to turn out the light, and that's when I noticed the envelope propped up against the lamp. Dad must have left it there for me after he picked up the mail this afternoon. Curious, I picked it up. I don't get all that much mail, and what I do get usually ranges from form letters telling me my subscription to *The Rodeo News* has run out, to advertisements promising that just ten fun-filled days with the new Flexi-Tense Exercise System will make me look like Arnold Schwarzenegger. Anyhow, I don't get much personal stuff in the mail—and this one was definitely personal. The pale-blue envelope gave me a strong suspicion it was from a lady.

No return address on the envelope, I noticed, playing detective. Then I checked the postmark, and that was all it took. *Nashville, Tenn.* hit me with a physical shock that felt like I'd grabbed a live electric wire. The letter was from my mom.

I stared at the envelope for a long time, lost in the rush of memories it released. Love and hate all mixed up together, so I could hardly tell which was which. I hadn't been able to sort it out back in the spring, and now I realized that a whole summer hadn't helped me come any closer to knowing how I really felt about her. Slowly I laid the letter back on the table. Whatever was in there could wait until morning. I couldn't handle anything else tonight. I turned off the light.

And five minutes later, I sat up and switched it back on. Who was I trying to kid? I couldn't leave that letter alone any more than an alcoholic could leave a bottle of booze sitting around untouched. My good hand was shaking a little as I tore open the envelope.

I spread out the paper. Two pages of delicate, slanted writing in fine, black felt-tip. A funny little shiver ran through me. That was the kind of pen I always wrote with too.

I started to read . . .

Dear Lance,

I know I'm breaking a promise to myself—and to you— by writing this. I said that the next move would be up to you, and that if I never heard from you I'd understand— and accept.

Well, I lied. I can't just ride into the sunset. It's been less than three months since I saw you, and already it seems longer than the whole ten years before. I keep thinking of how badly I messed up my one chance to become part of your life again. It's funny, but every time I think about what I did last spring, something your dad told me a long time ago comes to mind.

That was in the spring too. Mike had just brought the range horses in to halterbreak the new foals. I fell in love with one colt—a little black one—and I asked if I could train him. Mike said, "Sure," but when I started to walk right up to the colt, carrying the halter, Mike stopped me. "Slow down," he said. "Give him time, and when he's ready he'll come to you. But if you corner him and scare him, he'll run from you the rest of his life."

And that's what I did to you, didn't I? I came charging in with my big ideas of custody and tried to corner you.

And all I succeeded in doing was making you run from me.

Well, I know now that Mike was right about a lot of things and, whatever mistakes he has made, he still must be a great father. So I guess what I'm trying to do is say I'm sorry—to both of you. But I haven't got the nerve to say anything to your dad yet. Maybe some day.

My new album is doing really well and I guess I'll be doing a couple of tours this winter. Sometimes I get very tired of being on the road so much.

By the way, the picture you gave me is on my living-room wall. I'm looking at it right now. It's beautiful, Lance. Sometimes I wonder if you have any idea just how good an artist you really are.

There isn't much more to say. I guess it's pretty obvious how much I miss you. I do want to see you again very much, but on your terms this time. So when you're ready, come and visit, or I'll come up there if you say the word, or even a letter would help. Until then, say hi to Red for me. And tell your dad—tell him not to work too hard.

I love you.

Mom

P.S. How's the hand? I suppose by now it's all healed, but I still worry about it sometimes.

I read that last line and looked down at my hand. Yeah, I thought, you aren't the only one that's worried, Mom. And suddenly I caught myself wishing she were here now. So I could tell her how scared I was. So she could tell me not to be scared, that my hand was going to be okay.

Instinctively, as I thought about it, I tensed the muscles again, trying to make my fingers bend. But just like before, they barely even moved. It felt like they were made of chunks of old, rusty barbed wire, sharp-edged and so stiff they'd snap before they'd bend. Gradually the pain eased away—but the stiffness stayed.

I read the letter over again, trying to take in what it all meant—and to understand the feelings that kept threatening to sweep over me. My eyes were kind of stinging—from the light shining in them, I guess. I reached over and switched off the lamp but then just sat there on the bed in a room full of moonlight and tried to think.

There was still so much about my mom and dad that I didn't understand, but there were other things that now, for the first time, were beginning to make sense. Like why one of Dad's personal horses was a jet-black gelding named Ebony. Yeah, Ebony. I never could figure out where Dad got a fancy name like that for a horse. But I could figure it out now. It wasn't Dad that named him. . . .

And he'd kept that horse all these years. I knew he'd had offers to buy Ebony, and Dad hardly ever rode him. But he always refused to sell that horse. Was he still saving Ebony for . . . I stopped myself. Stuff you can dream up in the moonlight at midnight won't stand up in the hard light of the next morning.

I was getting cold sitting there. I lay down and, as I reached for the blanket, the Saint Christopher's medal that hung around my neck caught the moonlight. I'd been wearing that medal for so long it was like a part of me; I hardly even noticed it was there. But I noticed it now. Because Mom had given it to me when she left—the first time, when I was five. And in all the time she was gone, I never took it off. It was sort of like a magic spell, a special bond between us.

Last spring, when I first found out she was back, I'd torn it off and thrown it away. And good old Red had rescued it for me. I guess that's what best friends are for—to do your thinking for you in the times when your own brain gets all bent out of shape.

And now I was real glad I still had that medal. It was warm from lying against my skin, and it felt like an old friend. I went to sleep, holding it—smiling and feeling closer to bawling than I had for a long time.

12

I was tired Saturday morning when Dad called me at six, but his tone of voice told me this was no time to play possum.

Right after breakfast—which I missed on purpose, not being in a very sociable mood—we went to work on the truck. It didn't take long to confirm my suspicion that I wasn't cut out to be a mechanic. Pulling a motor, I discovered, is a hard, miserable, messy job—the kind where you scrape the skin off your knuckles, and the grease in your hair doesn't come from the drugstore. Maybe that's why I was kind of surprised that Kat was right in there helping, doing whatever Joe told her and, for her, acting downright meek. I noticed he didn't make any effort to spare her the dirty jobs, either.

We finished a little into the afternoon, and Uncle Joe decided it was early enough to head for the city to check out prices on some new motors. Four people in a truck seat is pretty cozy so common sense said that either me or Kat should stay home. I volunteered. I didn't want to go very bad in the first place, and I sure wasn't about to leave my territory—and my horse—undefended with her on the loose.

They'd been gone awhile and I was in the downstairs bathroom trying to scrub off some of the grease when there was a loud knock on the screen door. Muttering, I reached

69

for a towel, but then I heard Red's voice. "You home, Geronimo?"

"Yeah, in here," I yelled, and went back to scrubbing. Red didn't need an escort to find our bathroom. He came in, closed the toilet lid, and plunked himself down on it. He opened his mouth to say something, but I beat him to it. "You're out of luck, Paleface. She went to town."

"What?" Red said in an honestly surprised tone. I took my first good look at him then. Whatever he had on his mind, surprisingly enough, it wasn't Kat.

"Come on upstairs," I said. "I gotta find a clean shirt." I threw the one I'd been wearing in the general direction of the dirty clothes basket in the corner. It went in. Then I took a look at the towel I'd been using and threw it too. It missed. Oh well, in the famous words of Uncle Joe, fifty percent ain't bad.

We went up to my room, and while I dug through my dresser Red flopped down on the bed and stared at the ceiling. He was thoroughly bugged over something.

"Okay, Paleface, spill it," I said.

"Huh?"

"Don't play dumb with me, Red. With all the natural talent you've got, you don't need to fake it. So what went wrong? How bad did you lose?"

"Second," he snarled, slamming his fist into my unsuspecting pillow.

I sighed. "Paleface," I said, pulling on an old favorite holey shirt and flopping down on the bed beside him, "you're a real bundle of joy today. What's eatin' you anyway? Wasn't second good enough for your dad?"

"My dad," Red said slowly, and I noticed that his gray eyes had a hot, smoky look, "didn't go."

I sat up. "Didn't go?" I echoed, hardly believing my ears. Normally Red's dad is real competitive by nature, and when he gets involved in something he doesn't do it halfway.

He'd been so hyped-up over this race, I'd almost expected to hear he'd taken off running himself. "Why didn't he go?"

"Guess." Only one word, but the pent-up disappointment and frustration in it could have filled a book. I stared at him, not understanding at first. Then it hit me. There was only one thing in Red's life that could get him this tore-up. "Greg?" I asked.

Red nodded. "You got it, Geronimo. The hospital phoned this morning. Greg's sick."

I didn't get it. Sure Greg was sick. Red's brother had been in a coma for over two years now. I didn't figure you got much sicker than that. "What do you mean 'sick'?" I asked.

Red swung his legs over the side of the bed and sat up beside me. "He's got pneumonia or something," he said, and then added in a tight voice, "so they put him back on oxygen and all the other life-support stuff . . ." His voice trailed off, and he sat there silently torturing a handful of the fringe on the edge of my bedspread. Finally, he said, "That was Dad's idea, naturally. Two years and he's still waitin' for his miracle. Keep Greg alive—no, *alive* isn't the word for it, *breathing's* more like it—and go sit by his bed and hope." Red's voice was hard with anger—or was it disappointment. "And forget all about havin' another kid who just hangs around and gets in the way . . ." He looked up at me. "You know, Lance," he said, his voice softer now, "Dad almost had me fooled this time. I thought how I did in that race really mattered to him. I thought he was beginning to notice that I exist. But I should've known better. Sure, he might find a few spare minutes for me once in a while, but when the chips are down, he's gonna pick Greg every time." He stood up and turned to stare out the window, but not before I saw the tears in his eyes. I wished I knew what to say to make things better. I tried.

"Hey, come on, Red. Look at all the time your dad spent

runnin' with you and helpin' you train this summer. He cares what you . . ."

"Yeah, sure. And on the day of the race I had to call the coach and ask him for a ride, or I wouldn't even have gotten there to run at all. That's really caring."

"Look, Red. I understand what you're sayin'," I said, trying to cool him down a little. "But, I can see your dad's side of it too. I mean, if he really thought Greg might . . ." I hesitated—and Red finished the sentence for me.

"Die? Okay, then why doesn't he just do everybody a favor and get it over with? He had sixteen years of bein' Dad's favorite kid and another two of Dad's undivided attention as a reward for turning into a druggie and burning his brains out. What more does he want?"

I guess Red's own words finally registered on him because, all of a sudden, he stopped talking. He got this funny look on his face and, just like I knew would happen, the anger faded out of him and the guilt set in. Ninety percent of the time, Red's got a lot of common sense, but when it comes to the subject of his brother, Red loses it. It seems like he's on an emotional pendulum that can never hang balanced in the middle. It just keeps swinging out of control—anger, guilt, anger, guilt.

He dumped a couple of books off my chair and sat down straddling it and staring down at the Navaho saddle blanket I had for a rug. "That took a whole lot of class, didn't it?" he said, his voice real low. "The guy's worse off than dead, and I'm still jealous of him. That really stinks, doesn't it?"

"Yeah," I sighed. "It stinks all right, Red. But not for Greg's sake. He's beyond touchin'. But for you and your dad—that's something else. I mean, neither of you have got Greg anymore—not really—but it seems like you're tryin' to lose each other too. You and your dad and your mom, you're still a family . . .

"Oh come on, Lance," Red cut me off in midsentence. "You want me to go get my violin, or what? You sound like a rerun of *Little House on the Prairie.* Give me a break. You've been through enough to know better . . ."

I wondered about that, but I sure didn't need that particular conversation this morning.

"So, uh, Red," I said carefully, trying not to pull the pins on any grenades, "All this stuff you just told me, did you tell it to your dad too?"

He turned toward me, eyes angry again. "Yeah, I told him, more or less. Why shouldn't I? It's the truth, ain' it?"

"Yeah," I said soothingly, "It's the truth, I guess." Partly, anyhow, I added mentally. But I know, when it comes to Greg, Red's dad has a pretty low flash point. So I asked, "How come you're alive and well, then?"

" 'Cause, the referee stepped in, as usual." Red sat up straight and he didn't look any less fired-up. "You know," he said, angrily, "not once in my whole life can I ever remember my mom having an opinion of her own in one of these set-tos between me and Dad. Not once. I think I'd even respect her more if she'd take *his* side. But no way, not her. Is that all mothers can ever do—just stand around wavin' white flags and tryin' to keep fathers and sons from wipin' each other out—?"

"Don't ask me what mothers are supposed to do," I cut in. "I ain't exactly an expert on the subject."

Instantly Red cooled down. An embarrassed look crossed his face. "Hey man, I'm sorry. I didn't mean to—"

"Don't sweat it, Paleface," I said. "Anyhow, we're workin' on *your* case today." But then, since the subject had sort of come up, I couldn't help telling him. "I got a letter from her," I said. It felt strange to talk about it, like I should be keeping it secret, or something.

Red's eyes widened. "From your mom?"

"Yeah."

"No kiddin'?" he said, real interested. "So what'd she have to say?"

It was a hard question. I had that letter practically memo-

73

rized, but I wasn't sure I really understood what she was saying in it. I shrugged. "Nothin' much," I said, and then added, "and everything."

Red gave me a pained look. "You wanna translate that into something a white man can understand, Geronimo?"

I thought the question over. "I think she said she was sorry," I said at last.

Red grunted. "Well, she oughta be," he said.

"She also said hello to you," I added and, right away, the scowl that Red had been determinedly wearing ever since he walked in dissolved on him. "She did?" he said, and I almost thought he was going to blush. "Hey, how about that?"

I wasn't ready to talk about my mom any more just then, so I changed the subject. "You want to stay here tonight?" I asked. "Or won't your dad let you?"

Red shrugged. "He won't know the difference. He and Mom are stayin' in Calgary tonight at my aunt's place. Mom phoned and told me that after I got home. Greg's out of danger but Dad thought just in case . . ." The bitterness was back in his voice.

"Yeah? Well, maybe you should phone your aunt's place and leave a message, so . . ."

Red stood up. "Forget it, Geronimo," he said, suddenly angry again. "Look I'm not wastin' my energy helpin' Dad keep track of me any more than he wastes his time bein' with me. And if you've gotta make a federal case out of it, I'll just go home . . ." He started for the door.

"Red!" I yelled, and he swung around to see what was wrong. I heaved a pillow and caught him square in the face with it. "Shut up and get back in here, Paleface," I said. For a second he hesitated. Then he winged the pillow back at me, and we went at it.

By the time we were finished, the place looked like a chicken farm in a tornado; Red was cheered up; and since feathers always make me sneeze, *I* was depressed.

13

Sunday morning, Uncle Joe made breakfast—his kind of breakfast, which included steak and eggs and fried potatoes —and the smell of that cooking got Red and me downstairs fast. Dad was kind of quiet but that's normal for him, so I couldn't decide if he was still real mad at me or not. Anyway, Dad didn't need to talk much—Uncle Joe made enough noise for two people, thrashing around in the kitchen, like a clumsy bear banging pots and pans, and spilling stuff.

As for Kat, she was busy flirting with Red, which improved his mood a lot, and ignoring me. Then Uncle Joe announced that he was borrowing the Dodge and taking Kat to visit her mom's sister down at High River for the day, and I just about jumped up and hugged him. A whole day with Kat out of my life. Maybe Red and I could ride back to The Valley.

Then the phone rang. Dad got it. "Yeah, Ken," he said. "He's here. Spent the night. Didn't you know?"

Long, quiet space. Then, "Well, I'm sorry about that. Yeah, I can see how you'd be worried." More quiet. I glanced at Red. He was looking kind of sick. Dad's voice again. "Sure, I'll call him." Dad stuck his head around the corner from the hall. "Red, your dad wants to talk to you," he said in his usual calm voice—but there was something in the look on his face that spelled DOOM. Red and I exchanged looks. He stood up and walked into the hall.

"Hello?" he said, and you could have heard a mouse breathe in that kitchen as four of us sat there shamelessly eavesdropping. But a few seconds later we didn't even need to be quiet. You could have heard Red out at the barn.

"What for? You knew where . . . No, I didn't think it made any difference . . . Well, where'd you think I'd be? Kidnapped or something? . . . *Permission?*"—It came out more like an explosion than a word— "Dad, I'm fifteen. I don't need per—" Red didn't get that one finished. I couldn't hear the words but I could hear the pitch of his dad's voice, and I figured he had just straightened Red out on what he did and didn't need permission for.

"Okay, okay," Red muttered, quieter now, but still mad. "In about an hour . . . But we're just eating breakfast . . . No!"

By this time Red had the cord on the phone stretched out to its full length, and I could see him pacing back and forth like a nervous horse on too short a tether. "No! You don't have to come and get me. I'll be there in five minutes." He slammed the receiver down, and instantly four heads bent over four plates like four people hadn't heard a thing. The act wasn't necessary though. Red wasn't paying attention to what any of us were doing. He stormed through the kitchen without looking at anybody. Then, just at the door, he stopped and looked back. "Thanks for letting me stay here, Mike," he said to Dad—nobody calls my dad by anything but his first name.

Dad nodded. "Any time, Red," he said as Red flung open the door and disappeared outside. The rest of us sat there, not saying anything. When Red gets that upset, he always makes me think of a forest fire. All that red hair seems to blaze right out of control, and his face gets a hot look too. And then when his eyes go from soft gray to that smoldering, smoking color, watch out . . .

I figured maybe I better go see if I could cool him off a little. I looked at Dad. He nodded.

I caught up to Red at the end of the lane and fell into step beside him. He ignored me—which was good since I hadn't figured out what to say to him anyway. The first thing that came to mind was, "I told you you'd better phone your dad last night," but I talked myself out of that one. Finally I just said, "He was pretty mad, huh?" I didn't figure Red could argue with that.

He didn't argue. He didn't say anything.

I tried again. "So what'd he think? You'd run away from home or something?"

Red stopped walking and turned to face me. His eyes were still hot. "Don't kid yourself, Lance. He *knew* exactly where I'd be if I wasn't at home. He's just burned because he lost one tiny bit of control over me. Red moved without asking Daddy's permission. . . ."

I didn't answer that. Red didn't want an answer. He just wanted somebody to listen. We started walking again. "You know," Red began, not looking at me this time, "one of these times I really will do it. If that's the way he's gonna think all the time, he might as well have a reason."

"Do what?" I asked.

"Take off."

"What do you mean, take off? Take off where?"

Red shrugged. "It doesn't matter where. Just as long as it's outta here."

I stared at him. "Run away, you mean? Hey, come on, you wouldn't really do that?"

"Wouldn't I?" he said, and this time his voice—and his eyes—were cold. And that worried me more than the forest-fire look.

We were at his gate now and, suddenly, he turned and started to run up the lane. I wanted to follow. To explain to his dad. Explain what, I wasn't sure. Explain to both of them that they were driving each other crazy because they were both trying too hard? No, Red was on his own, I thought, starting slowly back toward home. He'd survive.

Anyhow, I thought tiredly, before I started sorting out anybody else's life, I had a little work to do on my own.

By the time I came plodding back into the yard, Uncle Joe was already in the truck and Kat was just opening her door to get in. Then she saw me. "Lance?"

"Yeah?" I said cautiously, walking over.

"Is Red in a lot of trouble with his dad?" she asked, sounding real worried. I looked at her, not quite sure I was getting this right. Kat was actually having a concerned thought for another human being? Then I reminded myself that the human being was Red.

"Yeah," I said, "a whole lot."

Her eyes went thoughtful for a minute and then she said, "Well, can't you do something about it?"

"Like what?" I asked.

She shrugged. "I don't know. He's *your* best friend. You should know. Talk to his dad, or something. After all, it's because he stayed over with you that his dad's mad. You should do something."

Well, that did it. Put things right back into their proper perspective. Kat might be concerned for Red, but her attitude toward me hadn't changed. If anything was wrong, I was to blame.

Uncle Joe was running out of patience. He leaned on the horn. Kat flashed him a nasty look that just slid off him like water off a duck. She climbed into the truck and he took off in a shower of gravel, yelling good-bye and waving—and barely missing the gatepost as he pulled onto the road.

Slowly, enjoying the quiet that had started settling in as the sound of the truck died away, I headed for the house. Dad was in the kitchen cleaning up after breakfast, and as I walked in, I suddenly realized that this was the first time the two of us had been alone together all weekend. I wasn't sure if I was glad or not. Any other time I would have been —but any other time I would have known how things stood between us.

I wandered into the kitchen and stood there sizing up the situation. No wonder Uncle Joe had been in a hurry to get out of here. Every dish in the house must be dirty. Dad noticed me standing there, and I soon found out that he was at least speaking to me. "Wash or dry?" he asked, looking pretty glad that reinforcements had showed up.

I shrugged. "Wash," I said. It's easier to fake it when you wash. Put the dish in the water, take the dish out of the water—and forget about actually wiping it with the dishrag. Works about fifty percent of the time.

I started washing and Dad kept bringing me piles of dishes. I was beginning to appreciate Dad's coffee-and-toast breakfasts more with each passing second. . . . I guess Dad's mind was running the same way. As he dumped still another load of knives and forks into the sink, I heard him laugh softly. "Been away from my little brother too long," he said. "Forgot rule number one."

I looked at him. "Rule number one?"

"Yeah. It says don't ever let Joe cook unless you got the kitchen door locked, or he'll skip out on the dishes every time." I laughed and started to feel real good inside. Me and Dad were okay. Maybe about the truck we weren't, but he wasn't going to freeze me right out on account of it. We could talk. Maybe it would even be worth a try to ask him about going with Uncle Joe. I'd work my way up to that one slow. . . . "Better hurry up with the dryin', Dad," I said. "I'm way ahead of you."

Dad threw the dish towel over his shoulder and flashed a triumphant grin in my direction. "Oh no you're not," he said. "I've been savin' this for a little surprise." He reached over on the stove and swooped back with the biggest, blackest, greasiest cast-iron frying pan that ever came out of the ark. I didn't know we even owned a thing like that.

The pan came to rest in front of my nose. "That oughta hold you awhile," Dad said.

"Hey, you cheated!" I said, laughing. Without thinking, I

reached for the pan—with my right hand. I could see it all happen like it was in slow motion. My fingers touched the handle, and Dad let go of it. A real normal thing to do—if you're dealing with a normal hand, that is. I felt the handle slipping through my fingers, and I tried to grab it. I really did. And in that same microsecond I tried to reach my left hand over there and get hold of it. But I ran out of time. The slow motion blurred into fast action and, before I could do anything to stop it, that heavy pan slid through my open hand and smashed into the sink full of dishes like a falling meteorite. There was a sound of shattering dishes, and then it was drowned out by the tidal wave of soapy water that leapt out of the sink to soak the curtains, the counter, the floor, me.

For a minute the room went dead-silent—except for the steady drip, drip, drip of water slowly falling from the counter to the floor. I didn't move. And from the corner of my eye, I could see Dad standing there just as still, staring at me with a look of stunned disbelief on his face. He didn't know. There was no way he could. I hadn't had a chance to tell him.

"What . . ." he began, his voice not angry, just puzzled.

I didn't wait for him to finish. "That hand's no good, Dad," I said, staring into the sink and managing to keep my voice expressionless. "I can't bend the fingers."

Dad didn't say anything for a minute. Automatically, I wrung out the dishrag and started slopping water from the counter into the sink with it. I could feel Dad's eyes on me, but I couldn't look back at him. When Dad finally did start talking, his voice had that guilty, helpless sound to it. The sound it always had when Dad figured that he'd somehow failed at being a parent—two parents. I hated it when he sounded that way. He didn't deserve to feel guilty. He was doing okay.

"I didn't know," he said slowly. "I should have gone with you to the doctor. I just thought it was like a broken arm or something. You'd get the cast off and . . ." His voice trailed off into a sort of helpless shrug.

I swallowed. "Yeah," I said. "Me too."

Dad kind of cleared his throat. "So, uh, what did the doctor say about it? It'll get better after a while, I guess, huh?"

I still couldn't look at him. "Maybe," I said.

"Maybe?"

"Yeah," I said. "That's what Dr. Meyer said. Maybe it'll get better in a little while, maybe it won't." This was a pretty weird conversation. In one way, I didn't want to talk about this whole thing at all. In another way, I wanted to keep talking about it. I guess I was waiting for Dad to come up with the old "Hey, don't worry. Everything's gonna be okay" routine, like most parents would have. But Dad didn't do that. Maybe it was because of his famous lack of "parenting skills." But I figured it was for the same reason he couldn't let Frank pay for repairing the truck. Dad had himself a real bad case of honesty. And he didn't know everything was going to be okay any more than I did. Then something else occurred to me. The fact that Dad was a totally physical person. All his life, Dad had made his living with his hands—two good hands. Finding out that I might have to get along with half of that had probably hit him just as hard as it had me.

When he finally did start talking, his voice was gentle. "Why didn't you say somethin' about it?" he asked.

This time I made myself look at him. "I haven't had too many chances to talk to you about anything this weekend," I said. I didn't mean it as an accusation.

Dad's weatherbeaten face softened a little. Slowly he shook his head. "You've had a pretty lousy weekend, haven't you, kid?" he said. I don't think he expected an answer. He didn't get one, anyway. Because, as he said that, he reached over, put his arm around me and hugged me, hard. And that did it. . . .

Because the rough stuff I can handle. Getting yelled at or hit, I can take that. Even the time Dad beat me with the lariat rope, I took it. I just clenched my teeth and stood there until he got tired of hitting me. And I didn't cry, either. Not until an hour or so later, when Dad had cooled down and he came up to my room and saw the cuts and bruises on me. I can remember the way he sounded when he spoke to me. His voice had that guilty sound then, too. "Oh, Lance," he said, like the words were being wrung out of him, "I didn't mean to do this to you, kid . . ." He started washing the blood off and putting some kind of cool stuff on the cuts, and I remember wondering how the same hands that could hurt you so much could be so gentle. And it was only then that I started to cry. Not because of the pain —although the doctoring hurt just about as bad as the beating—but because I knew Dad wasn't disappointed in me anymore, and I knew he loved me.

Now he'd gone and done it again. The minute he'd put his arm around me, my defenses all collapsed. Dad isn't the type of father who gives out hugs like jelly beans. When he hugs you, it means something.

Before I knew it, I had my wet, soapy arms around him, too. We stood there, like an island in all that spilled dishwater, just holding each other. And, yeah, I guess I did cry a little.

A minute later it was over. Dad gave me one last hard squeeze and then stepped back. It was man-to-man again. "You okay now?" he asked gently.

I swallowed. "Yeah," I said in a low voice—and I didn't figure I was lying this time. I wiped my hand across my eyes to get rid of the tears, got soap in them instead, and shed a few more, purely physical, tears over that. But on the whole, I was feeling a lot better than I had since I'd sat there, loud-mouthed and innocent, in Dr. Meyer's office on Friday.

Dad nodded. "Good," he said. He opened the cupboard

and brought out the old towel we use for a floor rag. "Then let's get this mess cleaned up." And, in one quick movement, tossed the rag at me. My reflexes came to the rescue and my hand—my left one this time, thank goodness—came up just in time to save me from getting that wet rag right in the kisser. I was getting to be a half-decent southpaw, I thought with something between pride and bitterness.

14

In spite of the start it had got off to, Sunday turned out to be a great day. After we got the kitchen cleaned up, Dad and I threw some bacon and eggs in our saddlebags and headed for The Valley to check on the cows we summer on the lease back there. It was one of those perfect blue and gold September days, and I could have stayed back in that country forever. We didn't talk much; Dad and I never do. But there wasn't much need for words.

But then, just like always, along came Monday morning. I staggered downstairs late, as usual, tired, and suffering from major depression at the thought of going through this routine four more times this week. Dad and Uncle Joe were already eating when I hit the kitchen. I fell into a chair and Uncle Joe poured me a cup of coffee. "Nothin' like a little brain food to get the school day off to a good start," he said cheerfully, happy as he could be to get me off to another day of torture. Altogether too happy. I wished he had to try spending the day folded up like an unused lawn chair, compressed into a desk made for somebody four inches shorter, and having to listen to the adventures of Hamlet and his Merry Men.

I looked around to see what there was to eat, and that's when I noticed Kat. She was standing by the stove, frying eggs, and looking for all the world like she knew what she was doing. "How do you like your eggs, Lance?" she asked, just as pleasant as a normal person. Well, *she* could afford to be pleasant. *She* wasn't going to school. She'd probably be out there riding my horse again as soon as I got out of sight.

"Cooked," I muttered grumpily. "And how come you're down here runnin' around loose in the middle of September, anyhow? You get kicked out of school already, or what?"

Kat smiled. It had to be her most irritating smile yet. "Eat your heart out, Lancelot. *Our* teachers are on strike."

"Yeah," Uncle Joe put in, giving me a wink. "Ain't that a shame? I been thinkin' about writin' one of them 'concerned-parent' letters to the school board about how my kid is gettin' deprived of her education—which is nothin' compared to the peace and quiet I'm gettin' deprived of by havin' to baby-sit her myself."

Kat took that comment as a challenge. She grabbed the first thing she could reach—fortunately it was a dish towel, not the coffee pot—and winged it at Uncle Joe. It missed him completely—Kat always did have a lousy aim—and landed smack in my coffee mug, splashing coffee all over creation, which included me.

"Ouch!" I yelled, jumping up from my chair. "Of all the stupid, boneheaded . . ." I went for her, dripping coffee and planning murder. But in two steps she was out the back door, running like a cheetah and looking back over her shoulder, laughing. I said a few words under my breath and turned back into the house, unbuttoning my shirt and pulling the soaking cloth away from my hide. It had taken me a long time to find a decent shirt for school, and with the bus due in five minutes, the chances of finding another weren't good.

I was still upstairs pawing through my dresser when I looked out the window and saw the bus way down the road. I grabbed a shirt—one I'd passed up a few minutes ago because of the big hole in the elbow—and took off, trying to put it on and take the stairs two at a time without killing myself in the attempt.

When I was almost at the end of the lane, the sound of someone calling my name caught my attention. I looked over my shoulder. It was Kat—with an armful of my long-forgotten homework. I pretended I didn't hear her and kept right on running, but just as I reached the bus, she caught up. "Here, Lance," she panted, out of breath but still talking loud enough that nobody on that whole bus could miss a word, "I didn't want you to get into trouble for forgetting your books." She smiled at me. It was the smile of a well-fed piranha. "Bye," she said. "Have a good day." She turned and strolled slowly back up the lane, looking as happy as a Girl Scout who'd just done her good deed for the day.

Oh yeah, I thought, for sure, Kat. You don't want me to get in trouble? If I were drawn and quartered and thrown to the alligators, it would make your day. For the first time in my life, I was almost glad I had to go to school. At least that was one place she wasn't.

I practically fell up the steps of the bus, shirt still flapping and books falling all over the place. The other kids on the bus had been taking in the whole spectacle and enjoying every second of it. A whole chorus of wolf whistles and "Ooooh, Lance"s followed me to my seat. Getting teased about a girl you like is one thing, but getting teased about somebody who makes Dracula seem cuddly . . . ? It was too much. Smoldering, I collapsed into my seat—only to have Johnny Hammer lean over from the seat behind. "Hey, Lance," he said, between smacks on a big wad of bubble gum. "You got better taste than I thought you did. Where did you get *her*?"

I turned around and glared at Hammer. I thought about smacking him a good one right in that hyperactive mouth. The mood I was in, I would have enjoyed it. But getting kicked off the bus wasn't something I needed to add to my list of problems. "Crawl back under your rock, Hammer," I snarled.

Then I turned to look at Red. He'd been dead silent through my entire grand entrance, and now I noticed that compared to him, a bloodhound would look downright cheerful. I nudged him in the ribs. "How, Paleface. Great chief has come. Why you not bring me greetings?"

He scowled. "Knock it off, Lance. I don't feel like playin' cowboys and Indians. I've already been scalped and burned at the stake."

"Meanin' what, exactly?"

Red turned to glare at me like the whole thing was my fault. "Meanin' I'm grounded for the next two weeks."

I nodded. "I was afraid of that," I said.

"What do you mean?"

"I tried to phone you yesterday, but your dad answered. He said—and I quote—'Jared's telephone privileges are temporarily suspended.'"

Red groaned. "He called me *Jared*?"

"Yup."

"Oh, great. He's even madder than I thought. He never even told me you phoned. I didn't get out of my room except to eat. I spent the whole, entire, complete day in there studying."

"Hey, man, the United Nations or somebody should get on that. That's cruel and unusual punishment."

"Tell me about it," Red moaned. "There we were, just me and Hamlet, locked up together . . ." Then he interrupted himself. "Hey, Geronimo, how'd *you* get along with the Prince? You understand Act One?"

I sighed. "It is with deep regret," I said solemnly in my best Queen Elizabeth accent, "that I must inform you that the Prince and I were unable to arrange a meeting over the weekend."

"You didn't get your homework done," Red translated. There was a long silence.

* * *

It started out to be a typical Monday at school. Most every-one, teachers included, spent the morning in a state of semiconsciousness, so I managed to slink through a couple of classes without getting too much of a hassle about my nonexistent homework. Oh, the teachers noticed it wasn't done, all right. I've got kind of a reputation for forgetting to do my homework, so they've gotten in the habit of look-ing mine over on a fairly regular basis. But once they'd made the horrible discovery, they didn't do much about it. Heavy-duty yelling takes more energy than most teachers have on a Monday morning.

At lunchtime, I had to settle for a vending-machine choc-olate bar. If Kat had to make that awful spectacle in front of all the kids on the bus, the least she could have done was skip the books and bring my lunch. And then, right after lunch break, it was time for *Hamlet.*

Tiredly, I folded myself into a back desk in Mr. Cartland's room and tried to line myself up directly behind a big person so I could be inconspicuous. The only problem was that I was about the biggest person in the class. . . . Oh well, if I was real quiet, Mr. Cartland might not even notice I was there. But, in spite of the fact it was Monday, he was acting dangerously alert. He didn't ask who had done their homework—twenty-eight hands would have shot skyward so fast you would have thought it was a stick-up. No, Cart-land took the sneaky approach. He started asking questions about Act One. And, what's more, he was asking the people who didn't have their hands up, wanting to answer. Now, that's what I call playing dirty.

He even asked Charmaine St. Clair—gorgeous Charmaine, with the face of an angel, the body of Bo Derek, and the brain of King Kong. It was amazing that anything that came in that fantastic packaging could be dumber than a sack of hammers. But Charmaine was. Had she read Act One? Well, put it this way. In her whole life, I'll bet

Charmaine hadn't read anything longer than the directions on a box of "Blond Beast" hair rinse. And, come to think of it, I wasn't so sure she'd even read that. She turned up at school once last year with her hair kind of a decaying-flesh green, and none of us could decide if she was trying to look punk or if she'd made a serious miscalculation in the directions. Still, even green, Charmaine had been kind of beautiful.

Suddenly, my mind jerked back to the present. I realized Mr. Cartland wasn't looking at Charmaine anymore. He was staring right at *me* and, from the expectant look on his face, I figured I must be supposed to say or do something.

But I just sat there pretending I was invisible. You see grouse pulling that trick all the time. They sit in the middle of the road and figure that as long as they don't move, nobody will notice them and they'll be safe . . . A lot of them get run over that way too, I thought gloomily.

"Lance?" Mr. Cartland urged.

I gave up and came out of hiding. "Uh, could you repeat the question, sir? I, uh, didn't quite understand it."

Across the aisle, I heard Red suddenly come down with a coughing fit.

"What I asked you," Mr. Cartland said patiently, "was what you considered to be the Prince of Denmark's biggest problem at the end of Act One."

I sighed. Whatever the Prince's biggest problem was, I had a bigger one right now.

Life used to be so much simpler, I thought wistfully remembering the system I had for bailing myself out of spots like this back in fourth grade. I always kept this big chocolate box full of pens and pencils and stuff on my desk, and whenever the teacher asked me something I didn't know the answer to, I'd just accidentally shift my elbow a little and knock the whole mess on the floor. I never did find a teacher with the concentration to remember where she'd left off after that.

But this wasn't fourth grade; the pencil box was long gone; and I still didn't even know who the Prince was, let alone what his problem was. Well, what the heck, if you're going to die, you might as well go out in a blaze of glory. I gave Mr. Cartland a big grin, shrugged, and said, "I think the Prince's biggest problem was that *Purple Rain* never did catch on in Denmark."

I had to stand in the hall for the rest of the period—but the look on Mr. Cartland's face was worth it.

15

It was only about ten minutes into last period when I heard my name called over the intercom. I did some mental calculation. The third week of school and I was getting my first invitation to the principal's office. Yeah, that was about on schedule. I hadn't lost my touch.

I headed for the office, wondering what Mr. Schafer had on his mind this time. I had a sneaking suspicion that three classes' worth of unfinished homework might be the subject. I wondered what he was planning to do about it. Once you got into high school, he usually gave up whacking you with the Board of Education. Probably I was in for a heart-to-heart talk with the principal—which meant that he yelled and I listened. Oh well, I'd survived worse. . . .

I guessed wrong. It wasn't Mr. Schafer who wanted to see me. It was Miss Cassidy, the guidance counselor. Interesting. I'd been hauled down here to be guided, not punished.

"Come on in, Lance," Cassidy called through her open door. I went in. She was digging around in her filing cabinet. "Sit down," she said over her shoulder. She pulled out a folder and came and sat down opposite me. She was looking pretty good, I decided, all tanned and with sun-bleached streaks in her dark-blond hair. I've noticed it before. Teachers always look better in September than in June. I wonder if there's a scientific explanation for that.

"Well," she said, smiling and supercasual, "how's it going so far?"

I wasn't sure what she had in mind, school or life in general. Either way, I lied. "Okay," I said, returning the smile. Wherever this little visit was headed, I wasn't planning on talking myself into anything I couldn't get out of.

Cassidy nodded. "Everything's cool, huh?" she said. For a teacher, she spoke the language pretty good.

"Yeah," I said, nodding too. When I'm lying, I do it with as few words as possible.

"I see," said Cassidy, and then I guess she'd had enough of playing catch with this conversation because she suddenly whizzed in a curveball. "In that case, Lance, maybe you could fill me in on the reasons why no fewer than three teachers have happened to drop in and mention your name so far today." She gave me her "teacher look." "Something about homework, I believe." She paused long enough to let me say something if I wanted to. I didn't want to. When your neck is already in the noose, squirming only tightens the knot.

Cassidy glanced at a piece of paper. "Yes, here it is. Biology, math, and, oh yes, English, especially English." She looked up and when her eyes met mine, the look in them said she was going to smile if she didn't watch out. "What did you do to Mr. Cartland, anyway?" she asked, the smile sneaking into her voice. "For a minute there, I was afraid he was going to reenact a Shakespearean suicide scene right before my eyes."

"Mr. Cartland takes his Hamlet pretty serious," I said.

"Yes," Cassidy shot back—I could see she'd gone and turned back into a teacher again—"and you could afford to take *your* Hamlet, and a lot of other things, a lot more seriously. Now, about the homework . . ."

Well, there wasn't much to say. I didn't have an excuse—not a good one anyhow—and I learned the hard way a long time ago that Cassidy's got x-ray vision when it comes to seeing through the phony ones. I shrugged. "I, uh, didn't get around to it," I said lamely, trying to look dumb and harmless. For a minute, Cassidy didn't say anything. She just sat there looking at me with that steady, unreadable expression of hers that makes me so nervous I'm soon ready to start confessing to crimes that were committed before I was even born.

Come on, lady, I thought, give me a break. Yell at me and get it over with, please.

But she didn't yell. And when she finally spoke, she sounded more tired than mad. "Lance," she said with a sigh, "do you have any idea how close you came to failing ninth grade?"

The sudden jump back to last June kind of took me by surprise, but the question didn't shock me any. Because by the end of final exams last year, I'd been *sure* I'd failed. So sure that when I read that "Promoted to Tenth Grade" on my report card, I couldn't decide if I was getting my Christmas present six months early—or six months late.

I guess I never have taken school as seriously as I should, but until last year the work had always come easy enough for me so that when the heat was really on, I'd dig in for a few days and manage to pull through. But in the last few weeks of ninth grade, right about the time when I should have been doing my magic act and pulling some decent grades out of thin air, my whole world had come unglued on me.

Between the Friday night in May when I saw my mom again for the first time in ten years and the June afternoon when Randy's knife landed me in the hospital, I didn't much know what I was doing. But I do know what I wasn't doing—my schoolwork.

And as if I weren't in enough trouble already, I got out of the hospital just in time to hit final exams. I got excused from all the essays and written stuff, and just had to do the multiple-choice parts. But that wasn't exactly doing me a big favor, 'cause multiple guess always blows me away. I remember how, halfway through the social studies test I just gave up and marked "c" for everything. Twenty-five percent was about as good as I could hope for anyhow, so I decided to get it the easy way. . . .

I glanced up at Cassidy and answered her question. "Pretty darn close," I said seriously. Then I threw in, "What are you tryin' to tell me? You teachers all got together and faked my marks to get me out of school faster?"

She laughed. "It wasn't quite that bad," she said. "We did have a meeting about you, though—"

"Yeah?" I said, getting interested. It was sort of an honor to be a big enough problem to cause a teachers' meeting.

"Most of us agreed that, considering the circumstances, your end-of-the-year marks weren't really fair. So we put a little extra weight on your first-semester grades and managed to squeeze out a pass. You know," she added, not quite hiding a smile, "for some reason that I often fail to understand, a lot of teachers like you. They really wanted to give you a break." The smile disappeared and she gave me a long searching look. "I just wish you had sense enough to do the same for yourself once in a while."

She delivered that one in a real quiet voice, but I still got the feeling I'd just been yelled it. It wasn't the kind of comment that's easy to answer. I looked down and wound my watch for a while. It was easier than meeting Cassidy's eyes.

"You've only got three years of school left, Lance. Then what? What are you going to do with your life?"

Wow! She really was into the heavy stuff today. I hardly knew about next week, let alone the rest of my life. "I don't know," I said, looking up. "Something outside, I guess. I couldn't stand bein' shut up in some office. Maybe I'll get a job like Dad's, workin' on a ranch. Or maybe try workin' on the rigs. They pay better. . . ." Or maybe, a voice inside my head sneered, you ain't gonna do any of those things. They don't hire too many one-handed guys for that kind of stuff.

Cassidy nodded. "No plans for college or anything like that?"

I laughed. "No, I ain't exactly the college type. If you ask Mr. Cartland, he'll tell you I'm already in way over my head." Then I thought of something I'd been wondering about. "Hey," I said, "what am I doin' in English 10, anyhow? Shakespeare and all that stuff is for the smart guys. English 13 is–"

I didn't get a chance to finish. "Lance," Cassidy said bluntly, "this isn't poker. Stop bluffing."

I blinked. "Huh?" I said.

Cassidy's look didn't soften. "You know what I mean. As a student, you're no prize—but it's not because you're short on brains. If you can't handle English 10, it'll be because you don't care. And you can fail English 13 for the same reason with considerably less challenge. Understand, Lance?"

I sighed. I hate it when somebody understands me like that. "Yeah," I said, tiredly, "I get the picture."

And suddenly she was off on a whole new subject. "Speaking of pictures," she said thoughtfully, "remember that one you did of Rowlff last year?"

How could I forget Rowlff? He was a real dog—any way you chose to use the word—somewhere between a Saint Bernard and a sheepdog, and with a face only his owner, who happened to be Cassidy, could love. He wandered down to our place one day, and while I was waiting for her to come and pick him up, I couldn't resist grabbing some paper and drawing his picture.

It came out pretty good—just as ugly as Rowlff himself—and Cassidy went crazy over it. Well, most of my pictures end up on my bedroom walls, and since there was no way I ever wanted to wake up and find myself staring at *that* face, I gave her the picture.

"Sure," I said, "I remember Rowlff."

And, ZAP! she'd changed the subject again. "Here, take a

look at this," she said, handing me a pamphlet of some kind. I looked at it. The Echo Lake Institute it said on the front, and there was a picture of a big, stone building way out in the mountains somewhere.

"Ever hear of that place?" Cassidy asked.

I hesitated, thinking hard. As far as I could remember, I hadn't heard of it. And even if I had, I didn't know what it had to do with this conversation. Unless maybe it was some kind of high-class reform school where Cassidy figured I was about to land if I didn't start treating old Hamlet with more respect. I stared at the picture. It was kind of gloomy-looking, but I didn't think there were actually bars on the windows . . .

I opened the pamphlet and gradually I caught on. The Echo Lake Institute was a college specializing in the fine arts. "It's an art school?" I asked, still not getting the connection.

Cassidy shook her head. "No, not *an* art school. *The* art school. The best in Western Canada. One of the best in North America. Here," she said, handing me a paper, "you might as well read what they had to say about you."

I looked at her. "About me?" I said. This was getting way too complicated.

"Read," Cassidy ordered. "Ask questions later."

I read. I skimmed over the page fast the first time, but then I slowed down and tried it over again. Groups of words kept jumping off the page at me and sticking in my head:

. . . definitely shows exceptional talent . . . special consideration . . . prepared to offer scholarship . . . outstanding potential . . .

I read it through a third time before I got up the nerve to look up at Cassidy and make sure I was really awake.

"It's on the level," she said. "That's really you they're talking about."

"But how . . ." I began.

She laughed. "You owe it all to Rowlff," she said. "I happened to meet the head of the Echo Lake art school at a conference during the summer. We got to talking about young artists and, well, I ended up sending her Rowlff's portrait plus a couple of other pictures you never collected from last year's art display. Then school started and I forgot all about it, until yesterday when this letter came in the mail. Of course," she added, "they didn't tell me anything I didn't know. I could have told them about your 'exceptional talent and outstanding potential' from that cartoon you drew of me on your notebook back in seventh grade."

I could feel my face start to do a slow burn, and I didn't know which was embarrassing me more, the compliments or Cassidy's overlong memory. When it comes to remembering things they should forget, teachers have got elephants beat.

Before I could think of anything to say, Cassidy said impatiently, "So. What do you think, Lance? Is the deal worth going for?"

I stared at her. I mean, did she even have to ask? The best art school in the country? And going there *free* because they thought I was *that* good? Me, Lance Ducharme, the big, dumb, half-breed kid who always drove the teachers crazy, drawing pictures when I should have been working on the important stuff. . . .

"Yeah," I said at last, real soft, almost afraid to talk too loud in case I woke myself up. "It's worth it."

Cassidy nodded. "Good," she said. "In that case, you'd better read Part Two." She pointed to *Prerequisites for Enrollment:*

All prospective students must have obtained a high school diploma in order to be considered for admission.

The words were big, but the message was short and sweet —mainly short.

"Get the picture, Lance?" Cassidy asked and her voice had gone stern.

I nodded. "Yeah," I said dejectedly. "I don't get in there until I make it out of here."

"Right. And that means the hard way, by graduating," she said. "And unless you start changing real fast, you're never going to get that high school diploma. You won't even last through tenth grade."

She let me digest that for a minute. It didn't go down any too good, but I swallowed it.

Cassidy lightened up a little. "Hey, come on, you aren't dead yet. School's just starting. You can catch up. Just try doing a little work for a change." She nodded toward my hand. "I see you've finally got that cast off so . . ."

And right then I *did* wake up. I should have known all this was too good to be true.

Art school? That was a laugh. What was I going to do there? Start all over at the beginning and learn to draw left-handed? I was lucky to even write my name left-handed. Or maybe, I thought bitterly, I could use my feet, like the people who do those Christmas cards you get in the mail. No way. The Echo Lake Insitute wasn't running a school for the handicapped. The only reason they'd wanted me was because I was good. Because—I corrected myself—I *used to be* good.

I guess my face must have gone white or something because Cassidy suddenly quit talking. "Lance, what is it?" she said softly, puzzled.

"Nothin'," I said, angrily, standing up. "I just don't want to go to that stupid art school, after all."

I wanted out of that office. I started for the door. I didn't need this garbage. Getting all your hopes up over nothing. I was going to get out of here and slam that door behind me and just keep running.

"Lance . . ." She didn't even it say it loud, but for some reason, it stopped me. I looked back. Cassidy was standing there staring at me. I sighed. Okay, I owed her an explanation at least.

Reluctantly I held out my hand. The fingers were half curled and stiff, like the claws of a dead bird. "The way this is, art school ain't gonna do me much good," I said.

At first Cassidy didn't say anything. She just came over and reached out and took my hand. I felt myself go tense.

"Hurt?" she asked gently.

"No," I said with a bitter laugh. "Not unless I try to bend it."

"But," she said, her eyes on my face, "this isn't as good as it's going to get?"

I shrugged. "Dr. Meyer doesn't know. It's all a big maybe."

"When did you find out it was like this?" Cassidy asked.

"Friday, when I got the cast off."

Cassidy let go of my hand. She shook her head. "And, on Monday I have to make your day with my big art-school surprise. Great timing, huh? I'm sorry, Lance."

I opened the door. If I didn't get out of here, Cassidy was going to have me bawling. And I'd never forgive her for that.

"It's okay," I said. "It's no big deal."

But as I walked into the hall, I knew I was lying again. It wasn't okay. Just once in my life I get a big break and . . . it wasn't okay at all.

16

I checked my watch. Almost time to go home. Too late to go back to class anyway, and I was glad. I knew I should at least stop at my locker and pick up my homework, but I didn't. I just went out and climbed into the empty bus, glad for a chance to be alone. But I wasn't alone for long. The bell rang and kids started piling into the bus. Red came staggering up the aisle, and he was carrying a double load of books again. He flopped into the seat beside me. "Hey, man," he panted, as he dumped a pile of books in my lap, "this is gettin' to be a habit. You too proud to carry your own homework, or what?"

I knew he was kidding. It was part of the usual routine between us, and he was expecting me to come back with a good insult of my own. But this time it hit me wrong.

"So who asked you to bring it?" I asked angrily.

He gave me a funny look. Then his red-head's temper let go. "Well, *excuse me,*" he snapped back. "I just had this weak moment when I thought it was okay to do a favor for a friend. Don't worry, it won't happen again."

I sighed. Man, was I being a jerk these days. "Hey, come on, Paleface, don't shoot. I'm sorry. I'm just in a lousy mood."

"No kiddin'" he said, and then he lightened up. "So what happened down at the office? Schafer come down on you real heavy about something?"

I shook my head. "Never even saw Schafer. It was Cassidy."

"Yeah? She's not so bad. What was bugging her?"

"Me. She told me I wasn't gonna last through tenth grade if I didn't smarten up and start workin'."

"That's all? Hey, my dad tells me that about twice a day. Here I thought it was something serious."

I looked out the window, so Red couldn't see my face. "No, nothin' important," I said. I was really getting into this lying business lately. But I couldn't tell him about the art school. Not now while the disappointment still hurt this much. Besides, he didn't even really know about my hand yet.

"So," I said, changing the subject, "how long till your dad eases up enough to let you come over to my place again?"

Red shrugged. "I don't know," he said gloomily. "From the way he was goin' on yesterday, I'd say about a million years." Then his face brightened up a little. "But maybe in a couple of days when he goes away. . . ."

"Where's he goin'?"

"I told you about that a long time ago. That law enforcement conference in Vancouver. He's been looking forward to it all year." Red's dad is a cop—*the* cop in Alderton, except for the RCMP.

I started to ask Red something about the conference, but the bus was already lurching to a stop at my gate. "See ya tomorrow, Paleface," I said, getting up.

"Yeah," he said. "Don't forget to do your homework."

I didn't waste my breath answering that. Then, "Hey, Geronimo?" I looked back. "Say hi to Kat for me, will you?" he said, straight-faced, and, to save my life, I couldn't decide if he was serious or just rattling my chain.

I gave him a look. "Believe me, Paleface, if I say anything to her at all, it'll be for you. I ain't speakin' to her."

Red just laughed.

.

And, sure enough, my chance to say hi to her came all too soon. She came galloping in from the pasture just as I walked into the yard, and, I thought with some satisfaction, the horse she was riding *wasn't* Spider. It was a half-broke three-year-old stallion that I would have rated the *second* most dangerous horse on the place.

"Hi," she said, sliding the horse to a show-off stop. I didn't say anything.

"How was school?"

"Thrill a minute," I said sarcastically. "Where is everybody, anyhow?"

"Aside from me, you mean?" she asked, her voice taunting.

"Yeah, aside from you, I mean," I said sourly.

The horse had about had his fill of standing in one place. He pawed the ground restlessly, then suddenly reared to his full height. Kat rode that out as effortlessly as if she were in a rocking chair and brought him firmly under control. "They went flying," she said. "Your dad's boss wanted him to take a look at a quarter horse mare that's for sale down by Lethbridge, so Dad took him down in *The Falcon.*"

"Why didn't you go?"

She shrugged. "Didn't feel like it. Why? You got some objection to me bein' here?"

I gave her a tired look. "Would it matter if I did?"

"Nope," she said, and pivoted the stallion on his hind legs and headed him toward the barn. "Those guys won't be back for supper," she called over her shoulder. "Uncle Mike said you could make some chili."

I stood there in the cloud of dust she'd left behind, not believing what I'd just heard. Now I was supposed to be cooking for her? Furious, I slammed into the house—only to be met by the irresistible smell of simmering chili. I followed it into the kitchen. There was a big pot of chili on the back of the stove, all ready to eat. And keeping warm in the oven, a pan of homemade biscuits. The table was already set for two. I was still standing there gawking when the door slammed and Kat walked in.

"You, uh, forgot your lunch," she said, maybe looking just a little embarrassed, "so I figured you might be too hungry to wait. Besides," she added, tossing her head, "eating *your* cooking could be hazardous to the health."

Well, war is war—but food is something else. So I let that one slip right by me and loaded up my plate.

Kat talked all the time we ate—mainly about horses. From the run-down she gave me, I figured she'd tried out about every horse on the place today. Then, all out of nowhere, "You see Red today?" she asked.

Dumb question. " 'Course," I mumbled around a mouthful of biscuit.

"Well, how was he doin'?"

I shrugged. "Okay, I guess."

"Is he comin' over tonight?"

"Can't."

"How come?"

"Grounded."

"For how long?"

"Dunno."

Kat thought a minute. I just kept eating. Amazingly enough, the chili was great. Then, "So, uh, what'd Red have to say?"

I gave her a blank look. " 'Bout what?"

Kat shrugged. "Oh, I don't know." Then she smiled. "Me, for instance."

I don't know why, but that was the last straw. I slammed down my fork so hard it bounced off my plate and hit the floor, taking a big gob of chili with it. Tomte, who'd been sleeping under my chair, jumped, sniffed, looked up, and, with a grateful "mrrup," accepted this unexpected gift from heaven.

"For cryin' out loud, Kat!" I exploded, "What is this, the Spanish Inquisition? You want to know about Red so bad, go phone him up or something. But leave me out of it. I ain't Dear Abby."

Kat's eyes started getting electric. She stood up. "So what's bugging you now, Lancelot?" she demanded sarcastically. "The fact that I happen to like your best friend? Well, just because he's got more class than you'll ever have in a hundred years, doesn't mean you have to be jealous of him."

I literally sat there with my mouth open. Jealous of him? Jealous? Before I could get the words out, Kat was gone, slamming the door behind her.

And there I was, left alone with homework and, sure enough, another big stack of dirty dishes. I did the dishes. I even considered the homework. I was still considering it—and reading a western paperback—an hour later when I heard that uneven engine sound that means airplane. I looked out just in time to see *The Falcon* touch down and come taxiing up through the hayfield. Good. At least they were home safe, I thought tiredly, picking up *Hamlet* and flopping onto the couch. "Something was rotten in the state of Denmark," it said. Well, to my way of thinking, things were pretty rotten in the province of Alberta, too. . . .

I was still trying to make sense out of that page when I heard Dad and Uncle Joe walk in. Uncle Joe leaned over and messed up my hair. "Hey, sunshine, how come you're lookin' so sour? You oughtta be celebratin'."

I didn't look up. "Celebratin' what?" I asked in a bored voice.

Uncle Joe laughed. "Your all-expenses-paid vacation in the middle of nowhere. What else?"

I sat up and stared at him, not daring to believe what I thought I'd just heard.

"Yep, I talked old stoneface into it," Uncle Joe said, giving Dad an affectionate poke in the ribs. I looked at Dad. He was smiling too.

"Dad?" I said.

He nodded. "Reckon I can spare you for a week," he said in a slow, serious voice. Then he gave me a wink. "Seein' as how poor old Joe just can't manage his big horse-drive without one of us along—so he says," he added, giving Joe a scornful look. "But"—and Dad's voice was real serious now—"you gotta make your own decision about missin' that much school. You know whether you can afford it better than I do. I'll write you a note sayin' I gave you permission, but the rest is up to you. You're the one who'll have to live with it if you get behind."

I'd like to be able to say I gave that decision a lot of careful thought. I did, too, for about thirty seconds—in which the ghost of Cassidy haunted me with visions of a wasted future. But I figured my future was about as messed up as it could get anyhow. Besides, this was the present. . . .

"Well, kid," Uncle Joe demanded, "You in or out?"

"In," I said but then something struck me. Uncle Joe wasn't taking me out for a pleasure ride. He was going to expect me to pull my weight on this trip. And I wasn't so sure I could.

"That is," I added, having trouble making myself say the words, "if I'd be much help to you like this." I held my hand out slowly and let him have a good look. "I can't use this hand," I said, wondering why I felt so ashamed to tell him.

Uncle Joe just nodded—but I caught the look that passed between him and Dad and realized I hadn't exactly given him a news flash. I wondered what the two of them had talked about up there in the plane all day, and I got a sudden suspicion that the subject might have been me. And I wondered just how hard it had really been for Uncle Joe to convince Dad to let me go. I was pretty sure he didn't need to have me along half as bad as he and Dad had figured *I* needed to go.

Uncle Joe gave me a scornful look. "That hand affect the way you sit on a horse?" he asked gruffly.

I shook my head. "No, but—"

I never got to finish. "That's what I thought," he growled. "So stop feelin' sorry for yourself and go get your bedroll packed. We're leavin' in the morning."

Getting told off had never felt better. "All *right*!" I said, and started for my room. Uncle Joe stopped me. "Why don't you see if your redheaded sidekick wants to come along? I guess you, me, and Kat can get the job done all right, but another rider wouldn't hurt."

I did a mental double take. I don't know how much of it showed on my face but, inside, I almost went into shock. Kat? He was taking Kat along on this ride? I don't know why, but it had never once occurred to me that she'd be there. It wasn't that I didn't think she could—cut it. Even in my most macho moments I'm not that stupid. Still, somehow I'd had this whole deal pictured like something out of a Marlboro ad—just us men against the wilderness.

Then I noticed that Kat had slipped in silently on her little Kat-feet and was standing there by the door looking at me. I had an eerie feeling that she knew exactly what I was thinking and that, inside, she was laughing at me.

I phoned Red. If his dad had answered, I probably wouldn't even have gotten to talk to him. But it was his mom; and, as Miss Cassidy would put it, "for some reason that I find difficult to understand," Red's mom likes me. We passed the time of day and then she called Red—no sweat. Either she didn't know he wasn't allowed even one phone call while sentenced to solitary confinement—or she didn't care.

Red reacted about the way I thought he would. He was real excited for me and real impressed that Uncle Joe had invited him too—but totally depressed because he didn't think there was any way his dad would let him even think about going. "Aren't you gonna ask him, at least?" I asked.

Red just sighed, but the discouraged look on his face answered the question he knew better than to ask.

I wandered outside after a while to tell Uncle Joe. I found him out in the field, tinkering with *The Falcon*. As I watched him adjust some vital-looking part of the plane's guts with a pair of bent pliers, it suddenly occurred to me that in about twelve short hours I was actually going to climb into that antique, and we were going to get a real long ways off the ground. I'd never flown before. What if it was as bad as that double-loop roller coaster Red made me go on at the Calgary Stampede last summer?

"Uncle Joe," I asked, "you ever get scared flying out there in the middle of nowhere in this old crate?"

Joe turned to give me an offended look. "Watch who you're callin' an old crate," he said. "There's a lady present." He gave *The Falcon* an affectionate pat on her weathered wing. Then he answered the question. "Scared?" he repeated with a big, lazy smile. "In *The Falcon*? That would be like bein' scared of my best friend. Nope, flyin' don't scare me none." He scratched his eyebrow, leaving a smudge of grease across his face. "You see," he went on, "the way I've got it figured, someday your number comes up and, when it does, you're dead. And stayin' away from dangerous places ain't gonna do one bit of good 'cause if it's your turn, you're gonna buy it—and fallin' down the back steps works just as good as flyin' into a mountain." He put the pliers away and rummaged around in his toolbox for a minute. Then he turned real serious. "Tell you what scares me a lot worse than the thought of checkin' out too soon."

"What?" I asked, wondering how I'd gotten myself into this conversation.

"Stickin' around too long," he said. "Livin' to be about ninety-five and gettin' to the place where the biggest adventure in life is tryin' to remember which way it is to the bathroom. Now *that* scares me." He stopped, looking kind of embarrassed as if he'd accidentally let me see a side of him that he liked to keep private. He bent over and went back to loosening a bolt, and I remembered what I'd come out here for.

"I don't think Red's dad will let him come," I said. The bolt suddenly let go and Uncle Joe barked his knuckle. He muttered something under his breath, and I wasn't sure if he meant the bolt, Red's dad, or both. Anyway, I didn't figure it was a compliment.

17

I didn't get a whole lot of sleep that night and what time I was asleep I spent dreaming—about that eighty-mile ride through all that beautiful, untouched country up there. And having nightmares about that five-hundred-mile flight through a lot of empty space in that cardboard-and-copper-wire excuse for an airplane.

But I was awake and ready to roll long before my alarm went off at six. My stomach was too full of butterflies for me to want to put food in there too, but good old Uncle Joe set a plate of bacon and eggs in front of me and when I tried to refuse, he growled, "Shut up and eat, or I'll leave you home." I ate.

I was almost finished when Dad came up from the basement with an armful of clothes he'd just taken out of the dryer. He threw them on a chair and unfolded a wrinkled piece of paper. "You never told me about this," he said, giving me a funny look.

"About what?" I asked, not having the foggiest clue what he was talking about. He handed me the paper. The first thing I noticed was that the printing was pale and blurry—which it usually is on papers that go through the wash. The second thing was the fact that it was on Dr. Meyer's office letterhead. At first, I just stared at it, not understanding. Then, it dawned on me. That day in the doctor's office, right after I'd freaked out over my hand. Dr. Meyer had tried to call Dad and couldn't get him, so he'd given me the note instead. Vaguely, I could remember stuffing it in my shirt pocket—and that was all I could remember about it. Right after that, I'd gotten all messed up with Kat and the truck and . . . The truck. I was still wearing that same shirt when we pulled the motor. I'd gotten it all greasy and thrown it in the wash. Now, I understood. But I didn't understand why Dad had picked this exact moment to get all hot and bothered about it. I had to be ready to go in a few minutes. I started reading:

Dear Mr. Ducharme:

Lance is suffering from some complications to his hand injury, and it is most essential that you and I talk as soon as possible. I have made an appointment for him to see a specialist in Calgary. If there is any problem with this appointment, we can discuss it when you come in.

Sincerely,
H. Gordon Meyer M.D.

Below that there was the name and address of the specialist:

Dr. Mitchell Tarrant
Suite 5, Lennox Building
Crowchild Mall
11 A.M. Sept. 16

I looked up to meet Dad's accusing eyes. He was mad and I didn't blame him. I'd managed to make him look like he didn't care enough about me to even call Dr. Meyer back. "I, uh, forgot all about that," I said honestly, kind of wishing the floor would open up and swallow me. "I'll explain to Dr. Meyer when we get back, okay?"

Dad's expression didn't change. "I'd call him right now, but it's too early," I added lamely, wishing he'd yell at me or something, anything but just stand there looking at me like that.

When he finally did break the silence, I didn't understand what he was talking about.

"Today's the sixteenth," he said.

I glanced back at the paper. Sept. 16. 11 A.M. He couldn't be serious . . . I shrugged. "I'll just have to skip it," I said. "Dr. Meyer'll get me another appointment if he wants me to see this guy so bad."

"No," Dad said.

No? I stared at him. What did he mean, No? He'd just let me miss a whole week of school without even turning a hair, and now he was saying no to missing a lousy doctor's appointment?

"Dr. Meyer called me a few minutes ago, while you were outside," Dad said, "just to make sure you hadn't forgotten about the appointment," he added, giving me a meaningful look. "He says this specialist is the best one around and that he'll come up with the best possible treatment for you. He also says this guy is booked ahead for months, and the only way he happened to get you in was because somebody cancelled an appointment. You can't just skip this one, Lance."

That was about the longest speech I'd ever heard Dad make, and I could tell by his face that he'd made up his mind. But so had I. I stood up. "No way, Dad. I'm not goin'. I'm not givin' up this trip to see any stupid doctor. I don't care what he's got to say," I said, my voice rising, "I don't want to hear it. . . ."

"Maybe you don't," Dad said in that quiet voice that sometimes fools people into thinking he'll back off if they push him, "but I do."

For a second or two, everything was dead quiet. But it was the kind of quiet that comes before the thunder and lightning finally break loose in a summer storm. Because I wasn't backing down. . . .

Uncle Joe's chair creaked as he pushed it back from the table and slowly stood up. "All right, all right," he said in the same calm but disgusted tone he'd use if one of his packhorses got his pack tangled up in the brush. "This ain't worth bustin' something over. You go ahead and see your specialist, Lance. It'll do you good to hear what he says and waitin' another day ain't gonna kill nobody."

Kat had been sitting there at the far end of the table, taking everything in. Now she heaved a big, impatient sigh and tramped off outside. Maybe Uncle Joe didn't mind being kept waiting . . .

Well, I went to Calgary, all right. Dad drove me down and neither of us said a word all the way. It felt funny. Dad and I never fight this way.

We got there right on time and, for his first act, this Dr. Tarrant kept me sitting in the waiting room for a full hour, which sure didn't improve my mood any. When he finally got around to remembering me, he started off by taking about twenty X rays from angles I didn't know had even been invented. Then, he hung up the X rays and showed me all the points of interest like he was a tour guide taking me through China. The only useful thing I got out of that was that all the main things that needed to be together in there were healed back together—in some kind of a way.

After that, he sat me down, took my wrist in a firm grip, and started bending my fingers back and forth, going "hmmm" to himself now and then, and asking me what I thought of the Stampeders' chances of making it into the Grey Cup. I didn't say anything about the Stampeders. I was too busy trying to decide if I should scream bloody murder so he'd get the message that he was killing me and quit, or hang onto my pride and pass out quietly. I was working on the second choice when he finally glanced up at my face. I guess I must have been looking kind of pale or something because he stopped bending my fingers. "That hurt?" he asked with a lot more interest than sympathy.

I glared at him. "Yeah, it hurts," I said through clenched teeth. "It hurts plenty."

His face lit up like he'd just won the lottery. "Good," he said. "Nerve function normal," he muttered, writing something on a piece of paper. I leaned back, took a few deep breaths and waited for for the sword fights that were going on inside my hand to die down a little. I wished I were enjoying this half as much as Dr. Tarrant seemed to be. Still, "nerve function normal" had kind of a good sound to it.

Dr. Tarrant wrote about half a page, put the paper in an envelope, sealed it, and wrote Dr. Meyer's name on it. "Okay, Lance," he said, handing me the envelope, "give this to Dr. Meyer on your next visit." He stood up and took a step toward the door. I had done the same before I realized that he was sending me home, and I didn't know any more than I did when I'd come in here. "My findings are all in that report," he said. "Dr. Meyer will . . ."

No deal. If it hadn't been for this guy, I'd be riding through British Columbia by now. He owed me more than this just for showing up. "I want to hear it from you," I interrupted, looking him in the eye.

The doctor sighed, gave me a look that was half irritation, but half respect too, and said, "Okay, I'll tell you."

Well, he told me—I guess. He talked for about five minutes straight about things like scar tissue, flexibility, loss of elasticity, psychosomatic factors . . . and a whole bunch of other four-syllable words that might as well have been Chinese, for all they meant to me. When he was finished, I still didn't have any answers.

"All I want to know," I said slowly, "is whether my hand's gonna get back to normal again. Did what you just said mean yes or no?"

For a guy with all that vocabulary, he seemed to have a lot of trouble with that simple question. He rubbed the back of his neck and thought a minute. "What it means," he said at last, "is maybe."

I walked out of there in a worse mood than I'd walked in —and that wasn't easy. The minute I got in the truck I ripped open Dr. Meyer's sealed envelope. I knew Dad was watching me out of the corner of his eye, but he didn't say anything. Not until I stuffed the letter back in the envelope.

"What'd you find out?" Dad asked, deadpan.

"Nothin'," I said disgustedly. "I couldn't read most of his writing and, what I could read, I didn't know what the words meant, anyway."

Dad nodded. "Could be why it wasn't addressed to you in the first place," he said, and a slow grin got away from him and curled the corners of his mouth a little.

I broke down and grinned back. "Could be," I admitted sheepishly.

On the way home, we passed Red's place just after the bus dropped him off, and he was plodding dejectedly up the lane. Dad beeped the horn and when Red looked around I gave him a big wave. From the look on his face, I knew I was going to have some explaining to do for still being around.

I was right. I was just walking through the doorway when the phone rang. It was him all right. He sounded kind of surprised to hear I'd had to see a specialist, but I got him off that topic as fast as I could and complained about how mad I was about having to postpone the trip for a day. His reaction wasn't as sympathetic as I thought it should be, but considering he couldn't go at all, I guess it was understandable. About the only good news he had was that his mom was driving his dad to the airport at the crack of dawn tomorrow, so he'd be able to get himself pretty well ungrounded for a while. Not, he added sourly, that it would help much. With me—and Kat—off in the wild blue yonder somewhere, there wasn't going to be much to do around here anyway . . .

I had trouble killing the evening. After all the excitement of getting ready last night, tonight was sort of a letdown. I was all packed and ready to go, so I just sort of hung around waiting for the day to be over. The mood must have been contagious because Dad seemed even quieter than usual; Uncle Joe lost himself in one of my western paperbacks; and Kat spent the whole evening curled up in the big chair with Tomte, filling his head with nonsense about how handsome he was.

It wasn't the alarm that woke me the next morning; it was Dad. "Lance!" he hollered up the stairs. "Red wants you on the phone."

I blinked a few times and looked at my watch. Red? At six o'clock in the morning? "Comin'," I answered sleepily, throwing on enough clothes to be respectable and stumbling down the stairs.

"H'lo," I muttered.

"Hey, Geronimo, can I still come?" Red chirped, sounding all bright-eyed and bushy-tailed like he'd been up for hours.

"Come where?" I mumbled groggily.

"With you guys, dipstick. Ask your uncle, willya?"

"But you didn't think your dad would . . ."

"Never mind, I worked hard on it and straightened things out. Stop wasting time and ask him."

Uncle Joe was just coming out of the downstairs bedroom stuffing his shirttail into his jeans. "Uncle Joe? Red wants to know if he can still come."

Joe shrugged and grinned. "Sure. Why not? Tell him to bring his long johns. It's gonna get cold up there these nights."

I turned back to the phone. "He says yeah—if you bring your long underwear."

"All right!" Red screeched in my ear. "I'll be there in ten minutes." He hung up before I could say good-bye.

Kat's head poked around the corner. She'd been eavesdropping, of course. "Red's coming?" she asked hopefully.

"What's it to you?" I said, just to make her mad.

It did. "Plenty," she said, tossing her head. Her eyes were the color of a sunlit thundercloud. I wished I could paint something that color.

Things started moving fast then, and an hour later we were standing out in the hayfield watching Uncle Joe stow our stuff in the plane. It was full daylight now, but I could see it wasn't going to be the bright, sunny, perfect summer day yesterday had been. The sky was a heavy gray, and it was plenty cool out there. A shiver went through me and I wasn't sure if it was from cold or nervousness.

"Okay, all you mustang-tamers," Uncle Joe was hollering, "let's get this show on the road!"

Dad stepped up beside me. "Have a good time," he said with his slow smile, and suddenly I realized that I was missing him already. I threw my arms around him and gave him a big hug. "Thanks, Dad," I said into his shoulder as he hugged me back. I let go and climbed into the plane fast, before I made a fool of myself. Folding my legs to fit the space in there was a major undertaking. Thirty seconds in that plane, and I already had claustrophobia. I heard Dad say good-bye to Kat and Red, and then he and Uncle Joe stood there looking at each other for a minute.

"Well, you crazy jackrabbit," Dad said at last. "You take care of these kids, y'hear?" Then he added gruffly, "Not that you've even got enough sense to take care of yourself."

Uncle Joe laughed. "You just stick to your cow sortin' and bale stackin' and fence mendin', you old dirt farmer, and eat your heart out when you think of how much fun you're missin'."

They both reached out and tried to squeeze each other to death in a bear hug, and I suddenly realized how special it must be to have a brother. Those two lived five hundred miles apart, saw each other every four or five years, and still kept a closeness that nothing seemed to change. For the first time in my life, I found myself kind of regretting being an only kid. But then it struck me that I might have had a sister—and she might have been like Kat—and I got over being sentimental real fast.

Red scrunched into the other backseat beside me, and Joe and Kat started to buckle themselves into the front seats. The engine sputtered and caught, and Uncle Joe revved it a little. "See you," Dad yelled over the roar, and then we were rolling across the bumpy hayfield, gaining speed, the pitch of the engine rising to a frantic whine and the plane's whole frame vibrating in sympathy.

The trees along the side of the field flashed past in a yellow-green blur, but the ones at the end of the field, directly in front of us, just kept getting clearer—and closer.

Suddenly Red's elbow jabbed me in the ribs. "How come you're so pale, Geronimo?" he asked innocently.

I looked at him. He was having the time of his life. To him, this was just as much fun as that double-loop roller coaster. Well, he'd flown half a dozen times before—in big commercial planes, that is. But for me, this was number one, and I suspected this wasn't breaking into flying the easy way.

"I'm always pale when my life's in danger," I muttered.

Red laughed. "Don't sweat it, Geronimo. Compared to that maniac horse you ride every day, this is dead safe." He could have picked a better adjective.

"Very fun—" I began, but at that instant the vibration increased to a violent shuddering and, with a lurch that came too close to sending me and my breakfast in different directions, we were in the air. The nose pointed upward at a steep angle, and I could almost feel that plane flapping its wings as it struggled for altitude. It reminded me of a time when, just at dusk, I'd seen an owl swoop down and grab a big rabbit and then try to take off with it. The owl wanted that rabbit real bad and he was flapping for all he was

worth, but almost too late, he had to give up and drop it—
and still he only narrowly missed crashing into the top wire
of a four-wire fence before he could gather altitude.

Then, all at once, the treetops were sweeping past below
us, their bright-colored leaves almost tickling *The Falcon*'s
belly.

"Yahoo!" Kat yelled, like she'd been single-handedly responsible for getting us off the ground.

Uncle Joe gave a terrible screech that stood the hairs on
the back of my neck on end. "Rebel yell," he explained,
looking around. "Learned it when I was in Texas."

"All *right!*" Red contributed, beaming all over his face
and not letting on it had anything to do with relief.

And me, I just swallowed hard and waited for my stomach to find out we were airborne.

Uncle Joe brought the plane around in a circle and came
in over the yard, rocking his wings up and down. Dad was
still standing there, a tiny, solitary figure, looking up into
the sky and waving. Then Uncle Joe pulled out of the circle
and we were away.

Once we leveled off, my stomach caught up to me and I
started to calm down some. If there had just been a little
more to that plane, I could almost have enjoyed it. But this
thing was too much like riding in a Japanese car with wings.
Still, the view from up here was something else. The pattern of the land took on a whole new meaning. It was like a
giant competition, Man versus Nature. All the farms
squared off into neat little blocks with straight roads in
between. Everything orderly.

And then along came the creeks and rivers and ranges of
hills. They went wherever they wanted, in curves and loops,
and messed up Man's neat little geometric designs something awful. I was glad they did. I always hated geome-
try . . .

We were flying west, and I suddenly realized where we

were. Over The Valley already. It takes a couple of hours to get there on a horse, and we'd been flying less than ten minutes. I looked down as we passed over the high ridge where the eagle lives. Whenever Red and I ride over the ridge, she always seems real proud that she can soar up there on the wind and scream down at us for invading her valley while we have to stay on the ground like low-class critters and put up with the insults. Well, I thought, now's your chance to come and get us, eagle. We'll have it out once and for all in your own territory, just like Snoopy and the Red Baron.

But she didn't show up. I guess she's got more sense than to mess with airplanes.

18

Nobody had much to say for the next hour or so. For one thing, *The Falcon* was a pretty noisy old bird, and yelling over all that racket got kind of tiring. Besides, we were too busy looking to talk anyway. There was a lot to see down there. Every now and then Uncle Joe pointed out a river or a town as we flew over it. I don't know how he could tell which they were. He sure never looked at a map.

We kept heading northwest, and in the country below us, Man and Nature were still battling. We'd go over some fields, a set of buildings, and then a big block of solid bush. Then more fields, irregular shapes with tamarack swamps sneaking in around the edges, trying to take back the land. A big, open meadow came in sight, not far from a set of farm buildings, and there was a herd of animals grazing on it. I wondered what kind of cattle they were at first, to be that color, but Uncle Joe got curious too and swooped down for a closer look. Then I saw the antlers. Elk. Close to fifty of them.

"Oh, they're beautiful," Kat said. "Wouldn't it be great to have a herd practically in your back yard like that?"

"That farmer won't think so this winter if they move in and start climbin' over all his hay bales," I said, remembering the year a big bunch took up winter quarters at our place and wrecked a couple of hundred bales. Elk aren't satisfied to just *eat* hay. To them, a stack of bales is kitchen, bedroom—and bathroom—all rolled into one, and once they've gotten into a stack, cows will starve before they'll touch it.

Kat gave me a disdainful look over her shoulder. "I should expect that from you, Lance. You can look at fifty of the most beautiful animals in the world, and all you think of is a little wasted hay. You've got the mind of a peasant," she announced, tossing her hair as she turned her back on me.

I just laughed. "Gee, Kat," I said, "just a couple of days ago you accused me of bein' a knight in shining armor. Now I'm all the way down to a peasant. How much lower can I get?"

"Not much," she said.

"Don't be too hard on the kid, Kat," Uncle Joe cut in with a chuckle. "Thinkin' like a farmer's contagious. His dad's come down with a terrible case of it, and I can see it's spreadin'. But a few nights of sleepin' out with the grizzly bears will straighten him out. . . . There's Rocky Mountain House," he said, interrupting himself to point out a good-sized town below. "And there's the North Saskatchewan," he added as we passed over the big river that slithered through the west part of the town, like a cold and sulky snake under the heavy gray skies.

Then the town was behind us, and ahead, nothing but wild country. This was still Nature's territory, and Man entered at his own risk.

It was maybe half an hour later when we hit the rain. Just little squalls at first. A darker piece of sky, a gust of wind, and a splash of drops across the windshield, and then out of it just as suddenly—only to start all over again five minutes later.

"Oh, great," Kat muttered. "We would have to get into rain."

"Yup," Uncle Joe sighed. "Figured we would. With that much cloud out in the open, you're pretty sure to find rain closer to the mountains."

Just then the plane gave a couple of little jumps, the kind

you'd expect from a goosey bronc on a frosty morning. "Okay, here we go," Uncle Joe drawled. "Sit tight, kids; looks like we're in for a little turbulence."

Turbulence, I thought. That had a familiar ring. Wasn't turbulence what planes always ran into just before they ended up splattered all over somebody's cornfield in those *Reader's Digest* plane-crash stories I always read?

The plane gave another little bounce and a crowhop or two, then smoothed out again. *This* was turbulence? I thought, feeling almost cocky. Heck, this was nothing. Spider could shake me up worse than this without even trying. I'd been expecting something bad.

All of a sudden, the plane shot straight up—yeah, *up*—with so much force the seat belt nearly tore me in half. I couldn't believe this. We were out of control. We were going to crash—what there was *above* us to crash into, I wasn't sure. I just knew that in seconds we were going to be history.

"Updraft," Uncle Joe said, wrestling with the controls but talking in a tone so casual I realized that this kind of thing must happen all the time. Then, before I could give that any more thought, the bottom fell out of the sky, and we dropped like a bomb. My head banged the roof, and my stomach just kept going up while the rest of me was going down. I swallowed. It didn't help. I swallowed harder. If these were my last few seconds of life, I wasn't going to spend them throwing up—I hoped. I managed to steal a glance at Red. He had his hand over his mouth and "paleface" had never described him better. I couldn't see Kat's face, but I got a good look at Uncle Joe. He was laughing at us. "Downdraft," he yelled over his shoulder, managing to outroar the wind and the engine. And even as he said it, we were back in smooth air. *The Falcon* leveled off and purred along like she was going down the highway. Uncle Joe turned around again. "So," he said, giving us a big wink, "how do you guys like flyin', so far?"

Well, for some reason I'd kind of lost interest in the scenery, and with the rain settling in steady, everything below was just a murky gray, anyway. I was so scared by now that all I could do was sit there and hang on, expecting another of those blood-curdling elevator rides any second. I noticed that, for once, neither Kat nor Red had anything to say.

We were flying through heavy rain now, and although that sure beat the turbulence, I didn't like it. Joe didn't seem very worried though. He got on the radio once—to where, I wasn't sure—and asked a couple of questions about the weather there. I couldn't hear the answers, but Joe didn't seem too happy with them. "Naw, it ain't that bad," he growled into the mike. "We'll get there. Might take a while though."

Not long after that, the first traces of white started swirling through the gray outside the window. Snow. Red and I exchanged glances, and I wondered what he was thinking. I don't think he'd figured on us running into a blizzard up here. I know *I* hadn't. I was beginning to have envious thoughts of those lucky kids back there on the solid earth, reading their *Hamlet*.

The snow got heavier fast, and visibility decreased just as fast. Kat craned her neck, trying to see the ground. "It's gettin' real murky out there. I can't see anything below us. Can't you get above this stuff, Dad?" she asked.

"Depends on how high it goes," Uncle Joe said calmly, "but we're gonna have to give her a shot. I've got the carb heat goin' full blast, and the snow's still clogging up the air intake. We gotta get out of the thickest of this before we start losin' power. And the only way out is up." He opened the throttle wide and poured on full power. "Come on, *Falcon*, baby, climb," he urged, sounding more like he was talking to a good old loyal cowhorse than to this coldhearted chunk of beat-up aluminum. Some *Falcon*, I thought, shivering as a gust of cold wind whistled in through one of her numerous air spaces. *Buzzard* would be more like it . . .

But the pitch of her engine rose, and shuddering a little harder, the old bird nosed her way slowly upward through the clouds. "Attagirl!" Joe's voice encouraged while his hand held steady on the control column. "I knew you could do it." And right then I realized that however much trouble we were in here—and all my instincts said we *were* in trouble —Uncle Joe was enjoying every minute of it. To him, it was all a game, like he had challenged the sky to a wrestling match and was planning to win. And seeing him controlling that plane and grinning like he was having the time of his life, I began to think he just might. As the plane climbed steadily through the storm, I started to relax a little.

Then, all at once, just like somebody had switched on a light, the inside of the plane brightened. I leaned my head way back so I could see out the window at an upward angle —and there it was: a jagged hole in the solid gray cotton of the cloud above us and just a little to the right. Through the hole, I could see a patch of clear blue sky and a brilliant shaft of sunlight pouring down. Relief came over me just like that sunshine. We'd made it, I thought.

But I thought too soon. Ever so slightly, the feel of the plane's motion changed. Then I knew what it was. We'd stopped climbing. I heard Uncle Joe swear softly. He slammed the throttle wide open again and the engine howled, but this time when he pulled back on the control column, the nose didn't lift. Slowly, gently, in spite of the straining engine, we started to lose altitude.

"What's the matter, Dad?" Kat asked, and I noticed there was more interest than worry in her voice. "How come she won't hold altitude?"

"Look out the window," Uncle Joe said. His voice was calm, but for once his face was serious.

We all looked—and it didn't take six months in flying school to be able to read the answer. Even in the dim, cloud-filtered light, the wings gleamed dully, coated with a thick layer of solid ice.

Kat put it into words. "She's iced up. She can't climb with all that ice on her wings."

Uncle Joe nodded. "I knew she was icing up, but I thought she might hold on long enough to make it to the top," he said, his eyes on the instruments in front of him. "But she's not even holding the altitude she's got."

"What are you gonna do?" I couldn't help admiring the way Kat asked the question. She didn't sound scared. She just sounded like she knew there was an answer and that Uncle Joe must have it. I wished I were that sure. It was downright cold inside that plane, but I was sweating.

"Only one thing to do," Joe said with a trace of his usual grin coming back, "and *The Falcon*'s doin' it for us. Lose some altitude, and hope it's warmer down there. If we can't fly over this weather, we'll just have to fly through it."

Then we were back in the snow. Really in it this time. I'd seen storms like this before. The early fall ones with the huge, lazy, aimless flakes that spin slowly down so thick they block out everything with a pattern of swirling white that leaves you totally disoriented. Dad and I drove home from Calgary in a storm like this once. It took us three and a half hours to do seventy miles. It was one of the scariest experiences of my life—and that was with four wheels on the solid ground and a ditch on either side to keep us heading in the right direction.

It had gotten real quiet inside the plane. Joe had given up his losing battle with gravity and eased the throttle back, so even the sound of the engine seemed muffled by the blanket of white that enfolded us. It was like being in a dream.

Crack! The sound was like a rifle shot, and instantly the dream turned nightmare. Another crack. And another. Something was hitting the plane all over, fast and furious, and bullets were all I could think of. I saw Red jump like he really had been shot, and Kat give a sort of startled squawk. My overactive imagination swept me right into the middle of every war movie I'd ever seen. This was like being in a tag-team dogfight with the Red Baron, the Viet Cong, and a couple dozen Russian MIG fighters, all rolled into one.

"Relax, kiddies," Uncle Joe's reassuring voice boomed through the gunfire. "That's good news you're hearin'. The ice is startin' to melt and the prop's throwing chunks of it back at us. We're okay now. She's levelin' off. Now if I can just get a fix on . . ." He started to reach for the radio mike.

"Dad!" It wasn't a scream, but something in Kat's voice made my skin prickle. And then I saw the reason. Dead ahead, close enough to stand out through the curtain of swirling snow, something dark. Big dark patches. Lots of them. Trees. The tops of tall spruce trees standing out black against the snowy hillside.

Uncle Joe reacted instantly. He hit full power and the engine screamed, but even in that same split second, he already knew.

"Get your heads down, and hang on!" he yelled, his voice registering more surprise than fear. "We're goin' in!"

I buried my head in my lap, an unbelievable number of thoughts rushing through my mind. Silently, I started to pray—and felt almost guilty for doing it. I really do believe in God; it's just that I can never think of much to say to him, and now it seemed kind of unfair to remember him when I needed a favor real bad. A line I'd once read somewhere flashed through my mind— "There are no atheists in foxholes." I wasn't sure I'd understood it when I read it, but it had stuck in my mind. *Now* I understood it. There aren't any atheists in airplanes that are going down, either. It was something I'd have to think about later—if there was a later.

I heard Uncle Joe's voice again, "Mayday! Mayday!

HOLD ON, GERONIMO

May—" The last word was drowned out by the screech of tearing metal, and I felt the seat belt grab me so hard it knocked the wind out of me. My head flew up, the plane bounced, and the world exploded.

19

I woke up slow. It was quiet and dark and cold. I wanted to go back to sleep, but Dad would soon be up. I'd hear his boots on the stairs, and the next thing I knew he'd be hollering at me to get up. Then the smell of coffee would come drifting up the stairs, and I'd come fully awake. Coffee. I could use some coffee right now, I thought fuzzily, shifting my head on the hard pillow. And that was my first mistake—moving my head, I mean. Because that's when I found out that somebody was inside it, trying to do brain surgery with a jackhammer. If this was a hangover, I thought, the night before *couldn't* have been worth it. I moaned and tried to drag the blanket of sleep back over me.

But how was I supposed to sleep with somebody shaking me? And none too gently, either. More like a dog trying to shake a gopher to death. My head . . . "Quit it!" I muttered angrily, "Leave me alone!"

The shaking stopped—and a voice started yelling in my ear. Red's voice. He must have stayed overnight at my place.

"Hey, man, you're alive! Geez, you had me scared." He kept on babbling away, but he wasn't making any sense. I'm usually alive, aren't I? Even first thing in the morning? What was going on here? I tried to think, but all my thoughts kept crashing into that pain behind my eyes and smashing into a thousand pieces. I reached up to rub my forehead, and my hand touched something warm and sticky. That got my full attention. Blood always does—especially when it's my own. My mind started to come into focus then, and I knew where I was. The plane. We were in the plane. It had gone down in the storm. I looked at my watch. It was working okay. Five thirty-eight, the digital readout glowed in the semidark. Five thirty-eight in the morning? We'd been here for over twelve hours.

I blinked at Red, who was still leaning over me like an overprotective hen. There was just enough light to see the shape of his face. It looked white. "You okay?" I asked.

"Yeah, I think so," he answered, his voice kind of shaky.

I stared at him for a while longer. I was still pretty much spaced, but it occurred to me that I should be real mad at him about something. Suddenly I remembered. "You ready to take that back about how safe this plane is—was?" I muttered sourly, struggling to unfasten my seat belt. It opened, and with a huge sense of relief, I discovered that I could get out of the seat. Nothing else was holding me, which was a good thing. I didn't figure I could handle being trapped in here. My next thought was to check on Joe and Kat.

I got carried away, forgot how little space there was, and tried to stand up. My head hit the roof, and a wave of dizziness swept over me. I sank back into the seat and the dizziness passed, leaving just that incredible headache behind. I groaned and edged myself as close to upright as I dared—carefully, this time. "Let's get the door open and get some light in here so we can see how Kat and Uncle Joe are," I said. There hadn't been a sound from the front seats and I was starting to get my brains unscrambled enough for that to scare me a little.

I started trying to push some twisted metal out of the way, but Red stopped me. "Hang on," he said, "my foot's caught under something." I bent over and tried to see, but there was only about two inches of space down there between the seats, and it was darker than the inside of a cow. I couldn't even find his foot.

"Got a match?" I asked.

"Yeah," he said, and a second later his hand touched mine. "Here." I took the match and tried to find a place to light it. I used to just scratch them with my thumbnail—till the head came off one and stuck under my nail, burning. I don't use that method anymore.

Finally, I decided the zipper on my jacket would have to do. The match was in midair when a thought froze my hand right there—and, in that same instant, Red's voice cut the silence. "Don't light that—" he began, and I finished it for him, "—'cause it'll blow us all to kingdom come." The air in there reeked with the fumes of spilled aviation fuel.

My hand shaking a little, I put the match away. That had been close. Too close. And for the first time, it really hit me. This was no game we were playing here. This was the real thing.

I reached down and felt around in the darkness. Finally, my hand touched something. The rubber sole of a running shoe. It seemed at a weird angle from the rest of the leg and it was caught under some metal. I gave it a little experimental pull and I heard Red gasp, but nothing moved.

"That hurt?" I asked.

"No," he lied. "Keep tryin'. Pull harder. Use both hands."

Yeah, sure, Red; great idea. I didn't say anything. I poked around some more, and decided that pulling wasn't going to help. There was no give to that chunk of metal, and I figured the leg had given about all it could while still staying in one piece. "It's not gonna work," I said. "It's stuck good."

"Come on, Lance, do *something*. Get me outta here." Panic was beginning to creep in around the edges of Red's voice. I didn't blame him, but I faked being cool. "Hey, come on, man, don't sweat it. No big deal," I said, trying to follow my own advice. If only it weren't so dark . . .

I kept digging around down there, mainly to convince Red I was still trying. Actually, I wasn't sure what to do. Then my hand came in contact with the top of his shoe, and that gave me an idea. He had on those high-topped runners that all the jocks wear, and they were pretty bulky. Maybe if I could get his foot out of the shoe . . . I found the lace, untied the knot, and unlaced it all the way down—and if you don't think that took a while left-handed in the pitch dark . . . As I did it, I could feel Red's ankle, hot and swollen, inside the shoe. All this pulling and twisting sure wasn't going to do it any good. But it had to come out.

"Okay," I said, "pull as hard as you can." I grabbed his leg and pulled too. Something had to give. I just hoped it wasn't anything too vital. All at once the foot came out of the shoe; Red gave a yelp of pain; and I landed in a heap on top of him.

"Red? You okay?"

"Mmmph."

I took my elbow out of his mouth and tried again. "Say something, Paleface. Your leg still attached?"

He never got to answer that because, just then, there was a soft moan from the front seat, and both of us froze. It was getting a little lighter now. I could see shapes silhouetted against the paler gray of the windshield. Everything was at a crazy angle. I could see now how we'd hit, nose first with the pilot's side taking the worst of the impact. That side was almost flat against the ground, while the door on the passenger side pointed toward the slowly brightening sky.

I could see Kat and Uncle Joe now, both still strapped into their seats. Kat was lying kind of sideways, but Joe was leaning forward, his head in his arms, resting on what was left of the instrument panel. He looked like he'd settled down there for a nap—except for the drying blood caked across the side of his head. He was going to have a pretty good headache too, I thought, automatically reaching up to touch the cut above my eye. Maybe we could make Anacin commercials together—when he woke up, that is. Which he'd better do right now, I decided, getting a real disturbing flashback of the scene they use in every movie that involves a plane crash. The one where, one second after everybody gets out, the plane blows sky-high. And with all that leaked fuel around here . . .

All right, just stay cool, whoever's doing special effects on this one. Don't jump the gun, okay?

Suddenly the moan came again, and this time I could tell where it was coming from. Kat. She shifted in the seat and sort of stretched like a person just waking up in the morning. She looked like she was going to be okay, I thought, but before I could even finish that thought, Red was crawling across the twisted seat to her. Whatever kind of shape his ankle was in, he didn't seem too worried about it just then. "It's okay, Kat," he was saying. "Everything's okay."

Leaning forward, I turned my attention to Uncle Joe. "Hey," I said, "come on, Uncle Joe, wake up and get us out of this mess, okay?" I knew he would; smacking into the side of a hill would be just a minor inconvenience to him, part of the adventure. I was looking back at Red as I reached out to shake Uncle Joe awake. My hand touched his shoulder—and jerked back. Like I'd touched something hot. Only it wasn't hot. It was cold. And stiff. "Oh, God, no," I whispered, feeling the grin go brittle and crumble off my face. He must have been dead for hours. Probably from the moment we hit the ground.

Slowly I turned to look at Red. He was staring at me. Huge eyes in a dead-white face. "Is he . . . ?" That was all he managed to choke out.

All I could do was nod. Both of us sat frozen with shock, staring at each other.

Finally I broke that awful silence. "He's never gonna have to worry about gettin' so old he has to ask directions to the bathroom," I said. It was probably the world's stupidest thing to say right then, but for some reason it seemed important to me. And if Red thought I was crazy, he didn't let on. He just nodded as if he understood.

"Dad?" a sleepy voice said. "What happened, Dad? Are we all right?" I turned to look at Kat just as she opened her eyes. She looked so young, a little kid, waiting for her dad to tell her everything was going to be all right.

I didn't want the next few minutes to happen. I would have done anything to keep them from happening. But it turned out to be Red who did all the right things. He leaned over and gently put his arm around her. "Just take it easy, Kat. We're gonna be okay," he said, and I admired the steadiness of his voice. "The plane went down in the storm, remember?" he asked, unfastening her seat belt.

Kat rubbed her eyes and sat up straight, looking around and wincing as she turned her head too fast. "Wow," she said, reaching up to rub her neck, "did it ever!" Then she noticed Red's arm around her. "I'm not in *that* bad shape, Red," she said, giving him a look that was half irritated but still kind of pleased. Then she firmly removed his hand from her shoulder. "Well," she said, her patience beginning to wear thin, "what's the matter with you guys? Let's get out of this thing. Where's Dad? Dad?" she said, raising her voice a little to make sure he heard her but still totally calm.

I realized then that she couldn't see past me to Uncle Joe, and I was glad. But she had to know.

I guess it was the silence after her question that told her something was terribly wrong. The tension was real enough to reach out and touch. All at once, she started to climb out of her twisted seat. "Listen, Kat . . ." Red began, his voice not much more than a whisper. But even it he'd been yelling at the top of his voice, it wouldn't have done any good. Kat wasn't listening. "Dad?" she called, louder this time but still under control. Then she was trying to push past me to get to Uncle Joe. I heard her take a fast breath, and I knew she'd seen him lying there. "Dad, are you . . ." She was on her knees, leaning forward and reaching around me, reaching out to Uncle Joe.

I grabbed her shoulder. "No, Kat, don't. You don't want to see."

She turned on me. "How do you know what I want to see?" she said in a voice that could have drawn blood. "Let go of me!"

I didn't and, like lightning, her fingernails sunk into my wrist and ripped. They *did* draw blood. I felt it warm against my cold skin.

I gave up. Nothing short of physically overpowering her would stop her now. And what right did I have to try to stop her? If it had been my dad, I would have had to see for myself. I moved out of her way.

"Dad," her voice was real soft. "Dad, come on, wake up." But I could tell from her face that she knew he wasn't going to wake up—ever. Gently she touched his face, and the words died away. She didn't scream. She didn't even start to cry. She just knelt there beside him, so still it was like she'd been turned to stone. Seconds turned into minutes. Nobody moved. Nobody said anything.

Finally, I couldn't take any more. "Kat," I said at last, my voice coming out kind of uneven, "there's nothin' you can do. There's nothin' any of us can do. Come on, let's get out of here . . ." She didn't answer. She didn't even move. I wasn't sure she'd heard me. I reached out and gently touched her arm. And instantly she reacted. She swung around to face me, her hands half clenched, somewhere between fists and claws so I didn't know if she was going to hit me or tear my eyes out. She was shaking.

"Don't touch me, Lance." She spat the words at me. "Don't you ever come near me again. If it hadn't been for you, you and your big-time drug-dealing knife wound, we would have left yesterday. We would have beat the storm, and right now we'd be safe at camp, and—" she hesitated, swallowed hard— "and my dad wouldn't be dead." She still wasn't crying. There were no tears in those storm-blue eyes. Only hate.

I stared at her, stunned, feeling like some kind of a criminal and not even understanding what I'd done. That doctor's appointment? The fact that Dad wouldn't let me leave on this trip until I kept the appointment? And because of *that*, Kat was blaming me for Uncle Joe being dead? Oh, man, I really needed that kind of guilt laid on me. Especially since, the longer I thought about it, the more I *did* start to blame myself. If only I hadn't . . . If only. Did anybody ever die without somebody who loved them saying those two words? And I loved Uncle Joe. It was only now that I realized how much. I'd probably spent only twenty days with him in my lifetime, but that didn't make any difference. You can be with some people all your life, and they'll still be strangers. Others are a part of you from the first time you meet. Uncle Joe was like that for me. And that didn't make it any easier to be accused of causing his death.

A voice was talking softly behind me, but it wasn't until Red touched my arm that I realized it was me he was talking to. "Hey, come on, Lance. She's so upset she doesn't know what she's sayin'. She didn't mean it," he said, quiet, so Kat wouldn't hear.

I looked at her, still crouched there like a cornered cougar; her eyes were blazing, but her face was cold. "Yeah," I said, my voice low, "she means it."

Red shook his head. "No. She just needs some time. Why don't you see if you can force that door open, get some air in here, and get rid of some of these gas fumes. I think it's safe enough here for a while. If it was going to blow, it would've done it a long time ago when the engine was hot."

I hesitated. "Go on, Lance, just back off long enough for her to get over the shock. She'll calm down. I'll stay with her."

Silently I nodded and turned away. I inched my way over to where I could reach the passenger door. It was slanted so nearly straight up that it took all my strength to push it open. I sucked in a lungful of the cold, pure air that came sweeping in. Then, with one last look over my shoulder, I scrambled through the door and jumped to the ground, almost landing on my face as the slick soles of my boots hit the snow-covered ground. The impact started my head pounding again, and a wave of dizziness swept over me. I grabbed the edge of the broken wing for balance and stood there looking around.

It was a world of white, like one of those Christmas card pictures—except in those pictures the poplar trees don't still have leaves on branches bent nearly to the ground with the weight of the snow. It was daylight now, but the sky was still that kind of dawn-gray color that comes before the sun rises. Then, even in the seconds while I watched, it started changing. Gray marbled with a hint of blue, then blue streaked with gray, and, at last, pure dazzling blue as the sun cleared the ridge behind us. To the east of us. My mind hungrily grabbed onto that piece of information. It was going to get real important to know which direction was which.

Then, as the sun flooded the hillside, everything lit up. The snow was so bright it hurt my eyes, and just enough breeze sprang up for some of the branches to start dropping their loads of snow. Their gold leaves stood out bright against a world of blue and silver. For a minute, I forgot how I happened to be here, and stood there just taking in those colors and falling in love with the country out here. I wished I had some paints. It was going to be a golden day. And right then an old movie title flashed through my mind. *Death on a Golden Day.* I couldn't remember anything about the story. I'd always just liked that title. But I didn't like it anymore. I hated it. Because for the first time in my life, Death had walked into *my* world and touched *me*.

Sure, I'd been pretty tore-up over a few good horses I'd seen die over the years—one of them I'd had to shoot myself—and I'd always felt a vague sort of sadness when a few hundred people were killed in an earthquake in Mexico or a plane crash in Japan, or something. Yet those disasters didn't seem quite real. They were so far away.

But this was so close to home it hurt. Physically. Like a wound way down deep inside somewhere where I couldn't reach it or do anything to make it quit hurting. I never realized that having someone die could be this hard to take. I mean, most people would probably think I'm one of the cold-blooded generation of kids raised on so much TV violence we don't feel much of anything anymore.

Well, if it's true, I ought to be their best example. Because I love all that wild action stuff, all the bodies and blood, and shooting and fighting.

But if anybody thinks that stuff has any connection to how it feels to sit beside a real human being and know that no matter how much you need them, how many things you meant to tell them, it's too late—they're never coming back . . .

I jerked my mind away. Stop it, I told myself. Keep this up and you're gonna fall apart. Don't think. Do something.

Do what?

Suddenly I realized I was shivering. It was probably as much from shock as from cold, but, still, in spite of that bright, early-morning sunshine, the air was plenty cool. A fire. We needed a fire.

I reached into my pocket and found Red's one match. There were more in the plane but, for some reason, it seemed important not to need them. I had to get the fire right the first time. I concentrated on that, shutting everything else out of my mind.

In five minutes the fire was burning perfectly—and I was back to not knowing what to do. I was going crazy out here by myself, and that just wasn't me. The only times in my whole life I can remember being real lonesome were when I'd been surrounded by people. But now I was lonelier than I'd ever been. I felt like some sort of an exile, like I'd done something so awful I could never go back to the real world.

All of a sudden, I remembered something that happened a long time ago. I must have been only about three then, and I was being a brat like only three-year-old can. Finally, Mom's patience ran out. She picked me up, carried me into the bedroom the way you'd take a misbehaving puppy outside, set me down, walked out, and closed the door. And I wasn't tall enough to open that door. I can still remember trying and trying, but always missing by just a little bit. I don't know what I was so upset about. Mom and Dad were in the kitchen, just down the hall. I could hear their voices if I quit bawling and listened. But that didn't help. I still felt trapped, shut out of the world where I belonged. Just the way I felt now, as I glanced back at the plane.

But back when I was three, the exile only lasted a few minutes. Come to think about it, that little punishment probably took as much out of Mom as it did out of me. Because suddenly she was back, picking me up and hugging me like I'd been lost for a week. I can still remember how good that hug felt.

Loneliness stabbed through me like a long, cold blade. I missed Mom so much. And Dad. And Uncle Joe.

20

It seemed like I sat there on a log by the fire forever, and the longer I waited the smaller I felt. This country could do that to you. Make you feel like you could disappear into the huge emptiness. Maybe we already had disappeared. All I had to do was turn my head a fraction and the plane was out of my line of sight. Then the forest looked like we had never been here. A few broken-off trees; that's all the difference we had made. We were the invaders here in Nature's territory, and I couldn't help wondering what she was planning to do with us.

Then, just when I was starting to imagine that I and a couple of curious whisky jacks that had lit in a nearby tree were the only living things left in the whole world, I heard a noise from the plane. I looked up to see Red carefully ease himself out of the door and come limping toward the fire. He'd managed to get his shoe out from under the seat and put it on, unlaced, but I could tell that ankle was plenty sore. He came and stood staring down at the fire, but he didn't say anything. I looked up at him from where I was sitting, but I couldn't think of anything to say either. Everything I was thinking was too hard to put into words.

Red held his hands out over the flames, warming them. "Fire feels good," he said at last.

"I nodded. "Yeah." And with the silence broken, I could ask the question that really mattered. "How's she doin'?" My voice sounded kind of rusty.

Red shrugged. "I don't know. She's so quiet. She just sits there starin' into space."

"Why'd you leave her alone in there?" I asked, a little accusation in my voice. I would have stayed with her—if she would have let me within fifty feet of her.

"Because she asked me to," Red said quietly. I nodded. That was reason enough.

Red shifted his weight, and I could see that his leg was bothering him. "Sit down and get the weight off that ankle," I said, brushing some more snow off the log and moving over.

Gingerly he eased himself down, keeping the leg stretched out in front of him. "You didn't bust it, did you?" I asked, worried. I leaned forward to take a closer look, but a stab of pain behind my eyes straightened me up fast. I leaned back against a tree and closed my eyes to let the world stop spinning. When I opened them again, Red was staring at me.

"You look awful, Geronimo," he said.

"Yeah?" I said tiredly, reaching up to rub my forehead and changing my mind. "Well, looks aren't always deceiving, Paleface."

"Let's see that cut," Red ordered, and I was too tired to argue. Obediently I turned toward him, and before I knew what he was doing, he'd scooped up a handful of wet snow and was washing the dried blood off my eyebrow with it. "Hey, watch it," I muttered, wincing as the cold shot through the cut.

"Sit still," Red said unsympathetically, reaching into his jacket pocket and pulling out a little first-aid kit.

"Where'd you find that?" I asked.

"Brought it from home," he said, concentrating on unwrapping some gauze. And right then, in spite of everything, I started to laugh. Good old Red was still playing doctor. Ever since he'd gotten the highest mark in the county on our eighth grade first aid test, he'd been having these delusions of doctorhood. It was real dangerous to get so much as a scratch because he'd be right there trying to cure you whether you needed it or not.

"What's so funny?" he asked, pouring antiseptic onto the gauze.

"Oh, nothin'," I said. He pressed the gauze against my eyebrow hard, and I jumped as liquid fire trickled into the cut.

"That cut's deep," Red announced. "If I were a doctor, I'd put some stitches in it."

This had gone about far enough. "Well, you aren't," I said, nervously, retreating a foot or so down the log, "so don't go gettin' any ideas. Just put a Band-Aid on it and leave it alone."

"Okay, okay, that's all I was gonna do." He slapped on the Band-Aid and then we just sat there again, staring at the fire.

A breeze had come up, and every now and then a branch would sway just enough to drop its load of snow with a muffled thud. Somewhere in the distance I heard a hawk scream, and that reminded me of the old Valley eagle—and home. The emptiness of the wilderness seemed to seep inside me, adding to the big, hollow ache that had already settled in my chest.

"So where do we go from here?" Red asked at last. I sighed. It was the right question, but I didn't have a good answer. "I don't know," I said. "Nowhere, I guess. Just sit here and hope somebody comes lookin' for us. The plane should have some kind of a homing signal that automatically starts working when it hits the ground."

Red shook his head. "It has one," he said. "Kat showed it to me. The only problem is that Joe forgot to check the battery on it. It's dead. And," he added, before I could ask, "the radio's completely smashed."

"That about takes care of everything, doesn't it?"

"Yeah," Red agreed. "It could take a while for them to search all the way along Joe's flight plan."

"*If* he even had a plan," I said, feeling kind of guilty just saying that, like I was betraying Uncle Joe or something.

Red's eyes met mine. "He wasn't very organized, was he?" he said softly.

I shook my head, and then added, "And even if somebody did know where he was *supposed* to be, he could have been way off course in that storm."

Everything got quiet for a while, and then I thought of something that would have been almost funny if it hadn't been so serious. "Your dad's sure gonna be sorry he broke down and let you come, huh?" I asked, thinking about how strict Red's dad always was. He sure picked a great time to ease up.

Red didn't answer for a long time. I threw another stick on the fire and turned to look at him. He looked strange, for all the world like he was going to be sick.

"Hey, man," I said. "You okay?" I figured he must be going into delayed shock from the crash or from his ankle.

"He didn't let me come," he said in a low, expressionless voice.

I stared at him, wondering if I'd really heard that. "What?" I said.

"He left for Vancouver yesterday morning and Mom was gone too, taking him to the airport, when I phoned you. I figured I'd just disappear, get on the plane with you guys, and, by the time Mom found out I didn't go to school, it would be too late for anybody to do anything about it."

"Well, Paleface," I said wearily, "you're right about that. It's too late, all right."

Red gave me such a sick look that I wished I hadn't said it, even though, for once, I was just telling the truth.

"It was so stupid," Red burst out, but I could tell his anger was at himself, not at me. "Just to get even with Dad . . ." He took a vicious poke at the fire with the end of a stick. "He's gonna be so worried. Both him and Mom. Dad'll never forgive me for this one." He threw the stick into the fire so hard that a shower of sparks flew up and came raining down on us like a horde of red-hot mosquitoes. Automatically, I brushed them off, but my mind was on how strange people are. I mean, to listen to Red when he's in the middle of one of his major rebellions, you'd think there was nothing he wanted more than to really shake his dad up, get his attention, and declare independence for all in one shot. But now that he'd probably succeeded in at least two out of three, it wasn't what he wanted at all. Growing up sure isn't easy. One minute you want your parents as far away as they can get; the next you wish they were there, holding your hand.

I wondered how my parents would react to hearing we were missing. Dad, that is. My mom wouldn't even know about it till it was all over—if she even knew then.

"Hey, come on, man," I said, bringing my mind back to Red. "Sure he'll forgive you. He'll be so glad to see you again." I grinned at him, and winked—not a bright move when you've got a big hole in your eyebrow, I discovered. "And *then*," I added, "when he sees you're all right, he'll ground you for the next hundred years."

Red groaned, but at least he came up with a feeble smile. I stood up to drag some more wood over, and as I did, that big hill to the east of us caught my eye again. Something about that hill had been in the back of my mind ever since I got out of the plane. Finally, I figured out what it was. "You know," I said, "with that high hill so close there's no tellin' what could be just on the other side of it. Who knows, maybe we're sittin' here half a mile from an oil well."

"Maybe," Red said, but he didn't sound very convinced.

"Well," I said, starting to feel better, "I'm gonna climb up to the top and find out what's on the other side. You stay here and take care of that ankle, and"—I glanced over at the silent plane and felt cold inside again— "see if you can get Kat to come out of there, at least." I turned and started for the hill without waiting for an answer.

The snow was melting fast as the sun got hotter, and walking up that steep hillside in slick-soled riding boots wasn't much fun. It was farther to the top than I realized, and it must have taken me close to two hours to get there. Winded, I stood leaning against a big pine tree and looking down the east side of the ridge. Looking down at—more trees. That's all there was as far as I could see. Which wasn't far, surrounded by thick forest like this. If only I could get above it . . .

Slowly my eyes traveled up the pine. It was a tall one. And it had big, sturdy branches that started low enough to reach from the ground. I hadn't done this for a while, but . . .

Well, one thing for sure, riding boots weren't going to do it. I pulled one off and stood there imitating a stork and considering my sock. No, it had to go too. Gingerly I stepped down onto my bare foot. Lightnin'! That snow was cold! I jerked off the other boot and sock and started up the tree. Ten feet up, I was having strong doubts about the theory of evolution. If any of my ancestors were apes, I sure hadn't inherited the climbing genes. This was hard. It seemed a lot harder than it had back when me and Kat used to . . . Kat. As soon as I thought of her again, a big wave of something that was both regret and anger swept over me. How come you're doing this to me, Kat? I mean, being the kind of enemies we were was sort of fun. But being hated for something I didn't do . . .

Suddenly my right foot slid off a wet branch, and for a second I hung there, one handhold between me and thirty feet of thin air. Gritting my teeth, I hung on for all I was worth, while my foot carefully searched for the branch. If my feet weren't so cold . . .

My toes touched the branch. Slowly my foot felt its way up onto it again. I worked my other foot up to the next

branch, cuddled my cheek up tight to the reassuring rough-
ness of the trunk, and clung there, shaking.

Yeah, I thought, this had been a lot easier before. I could
use both hands before. I stopped myself from thinking
about that. And about Kat. I couldn't afford to lose my
concentration again.

One handhold; keep your right arm around the trunk;
move one foot . . .

It took a long time, but finally I was as high as I dared go
—the tree was swaying every time I shifted my weight. I
wedged myself into a fork where the trunk split into two
tops and scanned the forest. Yeah, I was high enough. I
could see over most of the other trees. And as the country
below me rolled off into the distance in a pattern of green
and gold and white, I could see—more trees.

That was all, I thought, disappointment settling over me
like a wet blanket. All that work for nothing. But then
something caught my eye. Way off in the distance. An inter-
ruption in the sea of trees. Sort of a dark line that didn't
look like it should be there. Like, maybe, just maybe, a
road? Or a railroad track? Or a cut-line, at least. It was too
far away to tell, but I was sure it was *something*. And something is a whole lot better than nothing. I started shinnying
back down.

21

It was late afternoon by the time I'd slogged my way back down to camp. Camp. That was a pretty optimistic description of a fire and a crashed plane. But I noticed as I got closer that Red had been busy salvaging stuff. He'd dug out some blankets and sleeping bags and it looked like some food, too. He was sitting by the fire, and it seemed like he had something cooking. Correction, he *and* Kat were sitting by the fire. A wave of relief swept through me when I saw her there. She was getting it together. Kat was going to be okay.

But as I walked into the open, Kat looked up and saw me. And right then I knew that even though she had calmed down enough to leave Uncle Joe, Kat's feelings toward me hadn't changed. The look she gave me was so cold it burned. Then she turned away and stared off in the opposite direction.

Red spotted me too. "Hey, Geronimo!" he yelled and started to get to his feet, but changed his mind and sank back onto the log. "I was gettin' worried. What'd you find?"

"I dunno," I said, dragging up another broken chunk of tree trunk and sitting down on it. "Maybe somethin'. Maybe nothin'."

"Come on, Lance," Red snapped. "This is no time for one of your guessing games." Red's patience was plenty thin, I thought. But then I guessed mine would have been

146

too if I'd had to just sit there all day, waiting and wondering. At least I'd been *doing* something.

"Okay, okay, take it easy," I said, looking at Red but feeling Kat's eyes on me from across the fire. "I saw something way off to the east, a break in the trees. It could be a road . . ." Red's face brightened and I hated to have to dampen his hopes. "But," I added, "don't count on it. It was too far away to tell anything for sure. It could be where a forest fire went through a long time ago. It could be nothin'."

But once he had grabbed onto that little thread of hope, Red wasn't about to let go. "How far?" he asked eagerly, sitting up straight like he was ready to take off any second.

I shrugged. "Hard to say. Distance is deceiving up here. All I know is that it took me over two hours just to get to the top of that ridge, and this looks to be three or four times that far."

Red sank back dejectedly. "Too late to start today, then, huh?"

I looked at my watch. After four. "Yeah," I said. "It'll be dark in about three hours. We'll have to stay here at least for tonight." I thought I heard Kat take a fast, deep breath when I said that. I turned to look at her, but at that moment, the soup boiled over. Red grabbed for it, burned his fingers, pulled his jacket sleeve down over his hand, and tried again.

"Found some emergency supplies in the plane," he said, filling a tin cup and handing it to me. It was just that cardboard-and-sawdust instant soup, but right then just the smell of it was so good that my stomach practically sat up and howled. I hadn't eaten since breakfast yesterday.

Red filled another cup. "Here, Kat," he said, holding the cup out toward her. She didn't even look up.

"Not hungry," she said in a hollow-sounding voice. Red started to stand up, but I could see his ankle was really hurting. I reached out, took the cup from him, and carried it over to Kat. "Hey, come on, Kat," I said, gently. "You gotta eat."

I might as well have pulled the pin on a grenade. Kat leapt to her feet so fast she knocked the cup out of my hand and sent it spinning away into the snow. "I don't 'gotta' do anything you say, Lance!" she exploded, her eyes blazing. "You've already ruined my life. Just stay out of what's left of it." Head high, she spun around and stalked away from the fire. Stunned, I just stood there and stared at her, wondering how those few words could hurt so much.

Kat stopped over by the plane. She stood, head down, leaning against the broken wing, as if she were trying to get comfort from the old *Falcon*. As if it was all she had left now. I hated her for that. I didn't want to be the enemy. I wanted to be able to go over to her and . . . I didn't know what I wanted. I just wanted this to be all over. I wanted it never to have happened. I wanted to be eleven years old again, teasing hornets to impress old Cabbage Patch Kat.

I wondered if she was crying over there. I didn't want her to cry.

A hand touched my shoulder. Red was beside me. He was so pale his freckles stood out. I wondered how much of that look came from pain and tiredness, and how much was from the strain of trying to stay neutral between me and Kat. It seemed like Red was always getting caught in the middle.

"Hey, come on Lance," he said softly. "Don't let it get to you. It's not personal."

I turned on him. "What do you mean, It's not personal? She blames me, personally, for Uncle Joe gettin' killed, and she hates my guts for it. How much more personal do things get?"

"It's not you, Lance," Red said, his voice still quiet.

"Well, if it's not me, then why doesn't she stop blamin' me?" I asked, my voice rising in spite of my trying to keep it low. "Doesn't she think I feel bad enough about Uncle Joe without her—"

"She can't quit blaming you," Red cut in.

I looked at him. "What's that supposed to mean?"

"Hey, man, do I have to draw you pictures, or what? Can't you see that hating you is all that's holding her together right now? She's so tore up about her dad that the minute she lets go of all that anger inside her, the pain's gonna move in." He paused a minute. "And I think Kat would rather fight than cry."

I thought that over for a while. I knew Red was right about the last part. I hoped he was right about it all. That would make it a little easier to take. I shook my head. "She sure believes in doin' things the hard way," I said with a sigh, and took a swallow of lukewarm soup.

Red nodded. "Yeah," he said, "she does." Then he looked at me and added, "She's just like you."

I almost choked on the soup. "She's *what*?"

Red didn't even blink. "Yeah," he said calmly. "That's about how you handle things too."

I turned to face him dead on. Any other time, I would have shrugged that comment off without a second thought, but right now my nerves were shot and I didn't feel like taking anything from anybody. "Red," I said, "if you're tryin' to say something, say it. If you're not, drop it. But quit the in-between stuff."

Red met my look. His eyes were smoky, and I realized that he'd had about all he could handle today too. This was no time to push each other. But when Red started talking again, I realized that, for some reason, he really was deep-down mad at me.

"Okay, Lance, I'll say it. But you won't want to hear it. I'm sayin' I don't know where you get off thinkin' Kat's way out-of-line, actin' like she is, when you pull the same kind of thing."

"I *what*?" I interrupted angrily. "What are you talkin' about?"

Red didn't back off. "I'm talkin' about your 'silent Indian' routine," he said, his eyes on mine. "The one you pull whenever something's really got you tore up. The one where you just go into your own private world, lock the door, and don't let anybody else in." He paused a second, and when he started talking again there was more hurt than anger in his voice. "Not even your best friend. You know," he went on before I could say anything, "I always figured friendship was a two-way street, but I guess you don't see it that way . . ."

"What—" I began.

Red cut me off again. "Oh, when it's me that's got the problem, you're always there. But when it's you that's messed up, it's a whole different story. Then you turn into some kind of a comic book superhero. You don't need anybody. It's just you against the world."

I stared at him, completely stunned.

"And don't go givin' me that blank look, either. You know what I'm talkin' about. You did it when your mom came back . . ."

That really left me not knowing what to say. Because he was right. I'd been freaked out so bad over that whole deal that if Red hadn't hung in there no matter how bad I treated him, I don't know what might have happened. But that was old stuff . . . "Hey, come on, Red," I said, finally getting the chance to fight back, "that was once. Just once in all the time we've been friends."

"Yeah. And right now makes twice."

"What about right now?"

"That's what I'd like to know!" Red burst out, shoving a big stick into the fire so hard he pushed half the fire out into the snow. "That's the whole point. Something's been bugging you all week. You're so touchy that just talkin' to you's like shakin' up a jar of nitroglycerine. Something's wrong . . ."

"Okay, Paleface," I threw back at him, "since you know so much, *you* tell me what's wrong."

He hesitated a minute.

"Okay," he said at last. "It took me a while, but I finally figured it out." Real slow, so I'd be sure to get the message, his eyes left my face and his gaze moved down to my left hand, the hand that was still holding the cup. He glanced up again, just long enough to meet my eyes, and then his gaze settled on my right hand which, as usual, was holding nothing.

"Not usin' your right hand much, are you?"

I didn't say anything. He had all the answers. I waited him out.

Then Red's voice softened. "You can't use it, can you, Lance?"

I sighed, more relieved than anything else to finally have things honest between us again. Who had I been trying to kid, anyhow? Red was always able to see through my bluffs. I wouldn't even play poker with him anymore.

I shook my head, but I couldn't meet his eyes.

"But when I asked you the day you got the cast off, you said—"

I cut him off. "So I lied, okay?" I didn't even understand why I'd done that myself, and talking about it just made me mad.

I did look up then. I couldn't read the expression in Red's eyes. It wasn't anger. More like hurt—and accusation. "Why?" was all he said.

"I don't know," I said miserably, kicking a few stray coals back into the fire. "I guess I just didn't want to talk about it. 'Cause the more I talked about it, the more real it got. I couldn't tell myself it would go away . . ." The rest of the sentence faded out on me. I couldn't explain in words. Red would just have to understand; he always understood.

Only this time he didn't understand. He turned that accusing look on me again. "That's not much of a reason not to trust me. I mean, I know how you feel, but you could have at least . . ."

Suddenly my temper snapped. "Hey, man," I said, my voice rising, "what makes you think you know how I feel? You don't know how it feels until it happens to *you.*" I brought my hand up and held it, stiff-fingered, in front of his face. "You want the truth, Red; there it is. Take a good look. That's it. That's as good as it gets. Maybe as good as it's ever gonna get!" Somewhere, way in the back of my brain, I was already feeling like a fool. If self-pity showed up on radar, there'd be enough in the air here to have us rescued in no time. I gulped a couple of deep breaths and tried to make my voice stop shaking, but then I went right on talking. After all that time of keeping so many feelings dammed up inside me, there was no holding back now. "And I'll tell you something else, Red, I'm scared. 'Cause I don't know how to handle this. And I think I'm scared of being scared too . . ."—I added, feeling the spring inside finally unwinding enough to release the tension.

My voice trailed off into silence, and I stood there staring into the fire. I hadn't meant to say all that. Red must be thinking that crack on my head had jarred a screw loose in there. Embarrassed, I looked up. "That didn't make a whole lot of sense, did it?"

"Yeah," he said seriously. "It makes plenty of sense to me. I just didn't think it ever happened to you."

"You didn't think *what* ever happened to me?" I asked, more confused than ever.

"Getting scared. Feeling like things are out of control and not knowing what to do about them. That happens to me all the time, but you're different."

"What do you mean, I'm different?" I demanded, about half mad at him again.

Red hesitated. Then, "Remember the first day we ever talked to each other?"

A smile sneaked out on me. Did I ever remember! "You mean the day you decided you could outfight Brian Connelly?"

"Yeah," Red said sheepishly. "And you ended up having to rescue what was left of me. That's the way it's been ever since too. You're the one in control, the one that gets me out of trouble. Right down to that whole mess with Randy last spring. It's me he's threatening to kill, but it's you that jumps in and gets the knife away from him. Sometimes it makes me feel like Superman's sidekick or somethin'."

I shook my head. Man, was this kid mixed up. "So now you know," I said. "Superman's actually scared stiff."

"Yeah," he said, his face real serious, "Now I know. But I've still got one more question."

"Okay," I said cautiously, "let's hear it."

A slow smile spread across his dirt-streaked face. "Geronimo," he said, "we still blood brothers, or what?"

"What do you think, Paleface?" I held out my left hand. Red's hand met it—and just when I thought I might have to break down and holler, Red's grip loosened.

"Oh, great," I heard him mutter as he looked over my shoulder toward the plane. "Now what?"

22

Kat had found a backpack, from somewhere in the plane, I guess, and, the way it was bulging, she must have dug up something to put in it too. As we watched, she slipped the straps over her shoulders and bent down to pick up a rolled-up sleeping bag. I was afraid I knew what she had in mind. "What does she think she's gonna do now?" I muttered, starting to go over there and find out. Red's hand stopped me.

"Better let me talk to her," he warned softly.

I gave him a rebellious look. I was so sick of this. But remembering my last conversation with Kat, I gave in. I stood there and watched him limp over to the plane.

I couldn't hear what they were saying to each other, so trying to follow the conversation was like trying to watch TV with the sound turned off. There was a lot of hand waving and pointing. Kat pointed to the east. Red pointed to his watch and to the sun, which was already even with the treetops in the west. They were arguing. That much I knew. And Red was losing. That much I would have bet.

So I wasn't too surprised at Red's first words when he came back to me. "Put out the fire, Geronimo," he sighed. "We're movin' out."

I looked at him. "Get serious, Paleface. It's nearly dark; we don't know the country; and that leg of yours is good for about another hundred yards."

"Try tellin' all that to Kat," Red interrupted impatiently

and then added, "No. On second thought, don't. Just take my word for it—she's goin'. We've got three choices: let her go alone, try and stop her, or go along."

I thought those choices over—and put out the fire. We packed up the little bit of food and equipment Red had found and rolled up the blankets and sleeping bags while Kat paced around restlessly, wanting to get going.

I looked around one last time to see if we'd forgotten anything, and my eyes came to rest on the plane.

"We can't just leave him in there like that . . ." I began, my voice sounding hoarse.

"Yeah," Red said softly. "We have to. Kat and I wrapped him in a blanket this afternoon. With the doors closed, nothin' can get in there. It's the best we can do. . . ." His voice trailed off into silence. I still just stood there. Leaving Uncle Joe was admitting he really was dead.

Red touched my shoulder. "Let's go, Lance. Kat's already way ahead." Reluctantly I turned and we started east, up the hill again, walking slow.

Part way up the hillside I looked back, one last time, but already the plane was almost lost in the deepening shadows. It was just a broken bird lying dead in the forest and blending in with the white of the patchy snow. But one thing still showed up. There on the side of the plane the falcon flew as proud as ever, and the bright red letters stood out sharp in the rays of the sinking sun.

I could feel the tears burning behind my eyes, and I blinked hard to keep them back. It wasn't that I was ashamed to cry over Uncle Joe. He was worth it. It was just that I knew if let myself get started now, it would be awful hard to get stopped.

I glanced over at Red. He was walking as fast as his bad ankle would let him, and staring straight ahead like he really knew where he was going. But I noticed that his cheeks were wet.

And Kat just kept walking. She never looked back.

* * *

It was dusk when we got to the top of the ridge. It was time we stopped. I wondered what was keeping Red going. He looked nearly out on his feet. But out in front, a hundred yards ahead of us, Kat was already on her way down the other side. We followed.

A few minutes later, a sound caught my attention. "Listen," I said.

Red stopped and we stood silent for a minute. "Running water," Red said. "Must be a creek."

He was right. It wasn't a big creek, but it was fast and clear, and after all that walking the water looked good. The banks were slippery, so I helped Red edge his way down to the water before I lay down flat on my stomach and started sucking in water like a thirsty horse. Horse, I thought to myself, feeling a whole new stab of loneliness go through me. How come you're not here when I really need you, huh, Spider? The water was so cold it started my headache going again, but it tasted as pure as liquid crystal. Finally, when I'd drunk all I could hold, I stood up and took a look around. It was going to be pitch-dark before long. We had to find a place to spend the night. And just upstream, there was as good a place as any. I walked over to check it out.

There was an overhanging bank about eight feet high and, between it and the creek, a wide, dry gravel bar. Shelter and a place to build a fire. That was about as good as we were going to get tonight.

I turned and hollered over my shoulder to Red, who had just finished drinking, "Hey, Paleface, how's this look for a place to camp?"

Red looked over and nodded. "Anyplace where we get to sit down," he said wearily, "looks good to me." He looked over his shoulder to where Kat had been drinking a minute before. "Come on, Kat," he began, "let's get . . ." But he stopped right there. Kat was already gone, heading off downstream again. "Kat!" he yelled.

"We can make another mile or two tonight," she threw back over her shoulder and kept right on going. Even Red had about run out of patience with her.

"Kat, for cryin' out loud," he muttered angrily, turning fast to go up the bank after her.

I didn't see exactly what happened. It looked like he stepped on a loose rock, or maybe he just slipped on the muddy bank. Whatever it was, it threw all his weight onto his bad ankle. I saw it turn under him and heard him scream in the same instant. He crumpled to the muddy ground and lay there, not moving.

Then I was beside him, lifting his head and shoulders. "Red? Hey, man, come on, open your eyes. Talk to me, Red. You okay?"

He turned his head a little and blinked a couple of times. "Yeah," he whispered, "I'm okay." But it was his shock-glazed eyes that told the truth. If the ankle had been bad before . . .

He tried to straighten out his foot, and I felt him go stiff with pain. "Oh, geez, it hurts," he gasped.

"Yeah, I bet it does," I said, squeezing his shoulder. "Hang on. We've gotta get you outta here." As gently as I could, I picked him up—he was a lot heavier than he looked —and carried him over to the gravel bar.

Before I got him there, Kat came charging up. Even in the dim light I couldn't help noticing her eyes. They got real dark blue when she was worried. And she was worried now.

"Is he all right?" she demanded, trying to see over my shoulder.

"No, he's not," I said, not even looking at her. "Thanks to you."

For once, Kat had nothing to say. She just started un-rolling one of the sleeping bags and spreading it out in the shelter of the overhang. Red moaned softly as I lowered him onto it. I covered him with a blanket and then knelt down to have a look at his ankle.

There wasn't much to see. On the outside, the ankle looked about the same as it had this morning, except that now it was really swollen—so swollen that even the mostly-unlaced running shoe was tight on it. I started to reach down to see if I could loosen it some more, but Red's hand grabbed my wrist. "Don't touch it, huh?" he said. His voice was low, but there was panic in his eyes. The pain must have been pretty bad.

"Hey," I said, not knowing what to do—*I* sure didn't have any delusions of doctorhood— "if that shoe don't come off, it's gonna cut off the circulation."

Red raised his head and looked for himself. "If I get that shoe off, I'll never get it back on," he argued weakly.

I nodded. "You could be right about that. But I don't think you're gonna be walkin' anywhere for a while."

Red gave me a look that started out rebellious but powered out into resigned. He sighed and let go of my wrist. I started to reach for the shoe again, but suddenly Kat slipped in beside me. I guess she'd been looking over my shoulder all along. "I'll do it," she said quietly. "I won't hurt him as much." I couldn't decide if that comment was meant as an insult or a statement of fact. Either way though, I guessed she was right. It was a two-handed job.

"Let's see your jackknife, Lance," she said, holding out her hand without looking in my direction. I handed it to her, and she used it to make a long slit down the back of Red's shoe. Then, handling it as carefully as if it were glass, she started to ease Red's foot out. She was so gentle that Red hardly even twitched. I watched, fascinated, trying to understand how anybody that gentle could hate so hard. But then I reminded myself again that it was just me she hated. If I broke *my* leg, she'd probably want to shoot me to put me out of my misery.

I hauled in as much wood as I could before it got too dark

to see, and we built a fire on the gravel bar. It was going to be a cold night, I thought, as we sat there munching stale Granola bars and rock-hard beef jerky. None of it had much taste, but it didn't really matter. We were all so tired we were past hungry, anyway.

At last there was nothing more to do but huddle there under the blankets, me on one side of Red and Kat on the other, and try to keep warm until daylight. Nobody said much. The pain had eased off some, but Red still didn't feel much like talking, so that left me and Kat. Like I said, nobody said much.

Even huddled up together close to the fire with the blankets piled over us, it was cold. Too cold to sleep. Or maybe that wasn't why I couldn't sleep. Maybe it was because every time I closed my eyes, I could see swirling snow closing in around the plane, the ground coming up to meet us, and Uncle Joe . . .

I was still awake at two, but I guess I must have finally dozed off—until the screams woke me, that is. Kat. I doubted she'd ever screamed in her life when she was awake, but now I could see her sitting bolt upright in the cold moonlight. "Dad! Don't go! Dad, look out for—" Red leaned over then and put his arm around her. He shook her gently. "Kat, wake up. It's okay. It's just a nightmare."

Kat stopped screaming, and I could see she was awake. She took a deep breath. "No," she said in a hard, hopeless little voice, "it's not a nightmare. It's real." She turned away and buried her face in the blanket. It was a long time after that before I fell asleep again.

It seemed only a few minutes later that Red was shaking me awake again. I opened my eyes. It was dawn. Clear and cold. Groggily I sat up. At least my head didn't hurt so much today.

"Lance! Wake up and listen to me," Red's voice was somewhere between impatient and desperate.

"What?" I muttered sleepily, rubbing my eyes.

"She's gone. I woke up a minute ago, and she was no-where in sight."

I came wide awake fast. I stood up and looked around. Kat *wasn't* anywhere in sight. "Oh," I said with a lot more confidence than I felt, "she's around. She'll probably be right back."

"Yeah?" Red said. "Then why'd she take her pack and one of the sleeping bags?"

That about clinched it. She was gone. And that was all we needed.

Red and I looked at each other for a long second. "We can't leave her out there alone," he said at last.

I'd been thinking the same thing, but now I shook my head. "Forget it, Paleface," I said. "She made her own choice. We aren't goin' anywhere." I felt trapped. Whatever I did next, I knew it was going to feel wrong. "That ankle of yours has had it."

Red looked at me. "You're right about that. But," he added, *"you're* still movin'. Go after her, Lance."

"Oh sure, and just leave you here in the middle of no-where, alone with a busted leg. No way, Red."

"It's not busted," Red cut in.

"Well, it's as close as it needs to get. You can't stay here."

"For cryin' out loud, Lance, who do you think you are? My dad? Give me a break."

We stared at each other defiantly for a long time without saying anything, but somehow Red knew that he'd won. He reached into his pack and handed me a fistful of jerky. "She's got a big head start on you, Geronimo. Get goin' while you've still got snow to track her in."

I took the jerky—and gave in. There wasn't any choice. If something happened to Kat . . .

I stirred up the coals and threw some wood on the fire. There was lots of windfall around. At least Red could keep the fire going. I left him all the stuff, since I didn't want anything to slow me down. If I caught up to Kat, we were coming back here if I had to drag her. If I didn't catch up to her—I didn't even want to think about that.

"See ya, Paleface," I said, swallowing hard and forcing a grin.

"See ya, Geronimo." Red was grinning, but I knew he was scared. "Be careful, huh?"

"You too." I turned away, fast, and started on Kat's trail at a run. It was dead easy to follow. Even without the snow I could tell she was following the creek, so I mostly gave up tracking and followed it too.

Leaving Red like that was hard. The only way I could get that picture of him sitting there, alone and helpless, out of my mind was to push myself beyond thinking. So I just kept running. It was mostly downhill, but that didn't make it easy. The ground was slippery, and the creek ran through places where the windfall was so thick there was no way around. It was either over, under, or through those big piles of fallen trees. Other places, it was rocky and so steep that one wrong step, and I knew I'd be in worse shape than Red. I gave up counting how many times I fell. I just got up and kept on running. I was soaked with sweat in that heavy jacket, but I didn't dare leave it behind. Tonight it would get cold again.

Every once in a while, on a long, bare stretch of ground, I'd realize that I'd lost Kat's trail completely and, for a few seconds, I'd panic. But I still kept going, following my instincts. Stick to the creek, they told me, because that's what Kat will do. Kat might not be thinking too straight right now, but she knew the wild country and understood its rules. And one of those rules is to follow a creek downstream because finally—although it could be a few hundred miles if you're real unlucky—it will lead you to a bigger stream, and that will lead you to something else. A bridge, a town, eventually the ocean—that was an encouraging thought.

Sometimes I ran out of wind and had to slow to a walk for a ways, but I always broke into a run again. I had to find her.

I stopped and drank from the creek a couple of times and when I started to get light-headed, I dropped back to a slow jog and gnawed on some jerky. I checked my watch then. After one. I'd been on her trail for five hours. She couldn't be far ahead. I wondered how much farther it was to that break in the trees. I was beginning to wonder if I'd just imagined it. Because ahead, as far as I could see, there was nothing but tangled forest, unrolling out there forever.

I forgot about time. I stopped thinking. I was like a machine. Breathe in. Breathe out. Pick up right foot. Pick up left foot. Don't stop. Don't slow down.

It was so quiet. So empty. The sound of my own breathing filled my ears. Filled the whole world. Then, gradually, something else penetrated my red-hazed mind. I was hearing something besides my breathing. Water. That little creek was making a lot more noise all of a sudden.

I slowed to a walk—and then stopped dead. Because just ahead the trees suddenly thinned out and, through them, I could see, close-up, that dark line I'd seen from the top of the ridge. But it wasn't a road. It was a rock wall, a canyon wall. Suddenly I understood why the water was so loud. It wasn't the creek I was hearing. It was a river. A big one. That wall was its far bank. Disappointment welling up in me, I started walking over for a closer look—and then I saw something that stopped me in my tracks. A flash of red. A red jacket. Kat's jacket. There she was, leaning against a tree, looking out across the river. I went weak with relief. I'd found her.

23

For a minute I just stood there, letting the relief flow through me. I'd never in my whole life been so glad to see somebody. And that kind of surprised me. After all she'd put me through, why wasn't I mad at her anymore? Maybe I was just too tired, I thought. Stopping moving had been a mistake. My leg muscles were starting to quiver like half-set Jell-O. I started toward her again.

About twenty feet away I stopped. She was facing away from me, and I knew that she couldn't hear me coming over the sound of the river. "Hey, Kat!" I called, not too loud, trying not to spook her.

I still spooked her. She whirled around to face me like a startled deer. And looking at her, the last trace of anger drained out of me. Because if I'd pushed myself to the limit today, she must have pushed herself even harder. She looked like she'd been through a war. Her jeans were tattered and muddy, and one whole side of her jacket was ripped open. Through the torn leg of her jeans I could see that one knee was scraped raw, and underneath the dirt and scratches, her face was white. I didn't know what had kept her going this long. Hope, I guessed. Thinking that if she kept going long enough, somewhere she was going to find a way out. And, instead, all she'd found was a river that couldn't be crossed.

I understood. I'd been hoping too. But now there was nowhere to go but back. And it was going to be a long, hard walk. "Too bad, Kat," I said tiredly. "At least you tried. Come on, we gotta get back to Red before dark."

She didn't answer. She didn't even move. It was like she'd tried too hard, and now she was giving up. "Let's go, Kat," I said, real gentle. I held out my hand to her, thinking we were both too worn out to fight anymore. But I was wrong again. As I took a step toward her, she tossed back her tangled hair and her eyes flashed. "Leave me alone, Lance. I don't need any help from you." She took a step backward and—well, it all happened so fast I couldn't believe I was really seeing it.

In a single instant, the look on her face changed from defiance to confusion to terror. I stood frozen, staring, as the ground under her started to sink, then crack, then crumble. I lunged forward to grab her then, and instinctively she reached out for me.

Our fingers never touched. With a muffled splash, four feet of sodden, undermined clay bank collapsed into the river below, taking Kat with it.

And now, standing frozen with shock at the new raw edge of the bank, I really saw that river for the first time. From the sound of it, I'd known it would be a big, fast, mountain river, but there was something I hadn't counted on. With a foot or more of fast-melting snow all over these hills and a lot of rain before that, the river was in full flood. I searched the spot where, ten feet below me, Kat had hit the water. Nothing. The clay of the bank had dissolved instantly, and the few scraggly bushes clinging to it had already been washed away. And Kat was gone too. She didn't have a chance.

But even while I was thinking that, I was pulling off my boots, getting rid of my jacket, my shirt.

Fifty yards downstream, something caught my eye. I focused on it. A flash of red bobbing up in the foaming brown water. That was enough. I gulped a lungful of air and jumped.

I hit that water—and my brain exploded. At least, that's what it felt like. I'd expected it would be cold but not this bad. Liquid ice. So cold it stung. The shock knocked the wind out of me and, before I could get it back, the current caught me and was tumbling me downstream, out of control.

A chocolate milkshake. That was the first thought my numbed brain came up with. This was like being inside a giant blender, being made into a chocolate milkshake. The water looked like chocolate milk—but it felt like ice cream. I gasped for air, swallowed a mouthful of that water, and choked. It sure didn't taste like chocolate milk.

I surfaced again, sucked in another deep breath—air this time—and got it knocked out of me again as the river slammed me against a big rock. I'd lost sight of Kat, so I quit fighting the current and let it sweep me downstream. Just keeping my head above water was enough to take all my energy. Then all of a sudden, I caught another glimpse of Kat. It only lasted a second before the water slapped me in the face again and I couldn't see anything. But it was enough to see that Kat had her head up. She was still fighting—so far. But for how long? How much more of the cold and the current and the rocks could she take? How much more could *I* take?

I started swimming along with the current—if you could call it swimming. Mostly I was bouncing off rocks or drift-wood, dragging bottom one second, not even able to touch it the next. But I kept kicking, and the next time I saw Kat's red jacket, it was closer.

I don't know how long it went on—the swimming and going under and surfacing and getting slammed against stuff and swallowing water and trying to breathe. It felt like forever. Like being in a real bad dream where you know you've got to wake yourself up if you want to get out alive—but you can't wake up. Really, though, it must have been only a few minutes. That was as long as either one of us would have lasted.

Then the river swept into a big bend, and the current seemed to slow down a little. This time when I raised my head, Kat was just a few yards ahead of me. "Kat!" I screamed at the top of my voice, and I saw her glance back over her shoulder. I wasn't sure, but I thought she saw me. Before I could holler again, we were into more rocks. Big ones, this time. They must have stood almost clear of the water when it was at a normal level. Even now their tops broke the surface.

"Kat!" I yelled again, as the current swept her between those huge rocks. "Grab the rock and hang on!" What I was asking was impossible, and I knew it. Nobody could hang on to the side of a smooth, wet rock with their fingers numb and the current tearing at them.

But Kat did it. For about three seconds. And that was all it took. I was beside her then and my left hand brushed her sleeve. I grabbed onto it just as she lost her hold on the slippery rock. Kat's eyes met mine for a second. "Pretty dumb to jump in, Lancelot," she gasped, fighting to keep her face out of the water.

"Wouldn't have to if you'd learn to swim," I managed to say as the current tore us away again. The world turned back into a dream. A wild roller-coaster ride, colors flashing by. Brown water, blue sky, green trees, white patches of snow.

I don't know how far downstream that water carried us, but dimly I began to notice a change. The banks weren't so high anymore. Only about three feet in places. We could get out now. Yeah, sure we could get out, *if* we could get *to* the bank. But I didn't figure I was going to make it to the bank—or anywhere else. My whole body was going dead from the cold. My fingers were so numb that I had to look to make sure I still had hold of Kat's jacket. I tried to kick out of the drag of the current and angle toward shore, but my legs were too heavy. Now it was like trying to swim through freezing molasses. I looked at Kat. Her eyes were closed. "Open your eyes, Kat!" I yelled in her ear. "Don't you give up on me now!" She opened her eyes, but I couldn't stand the look in them. She knew we weren't going to make it. I turned away, and that's when I saw the tree.

It was a big spruce, half uprooted and leaning way out over the river at an angle so low that its bottom branches swept the water. That farthest-out branch. The current was going to bring us close. It was a chance, our only chance. . . .

It was coming up fast. I took a big gulp of air that turned out to be half water, coughed, gulped again, and kicked as hard as I could. Instantly Kat understood. I felt her kick too. The current fought us like a lassoed calf, but we gained a foot, another . . . One more kick. This had to do it. I didn't have another kick in me.

I reached for the branch and my hand touched something rough. Spruce bark! We'd made it. From here we could work our way along the tree to the bank. All I had to do was hold on to that branch.

And then reality hit me. I *couldn't* hold on to the branch. Not with that hand. And I couldn't let go of Kat to use my left one. She wasn't close enough to grab the branch herself. If I let go, she'd get swept away again. I felt the rough bark sliding through my open hand. I was losing it. Our one chance was literally slipping through my fingers. No! It wasn't fair. I'd tried too hard. I didn't deserve this. Kat didn't deserve this.

Suddenly all the disappointment and frustration that had been building up inside me broke loose with a wildfire fury that flashed through me, burning away everything in its path. Even the icy numbness in me seemed to retreat a little as my brain screamed a silent message to my body. Grab the branch! Grab it or die! And take Kat with you. Let her die too. And this time it *will* be your fault. You're the only one who can save her and you're blowin' it. Grab the branch!

I can't.

Do it.

I tried to make my fingers bend. But I couldn't do it. It was like trying to crush a handful of broken glass.

I can't. It hurts too much . . .

You think dyin's gonna feel great?

The whole world centered in on one dead spruce branch and that throbbing, quivering hand. It had to bend. It had to . . .

Suddenly somewhere inside there, a grenade of pain exploded. I screamed—and felt water burning in my lungs. Darkness flowed over me.

24

Consciousness seeped back into my mind like the first pale light of dawn edging across a dark sky. My fog-drenched brain struggled toward the light, and I tried to bring things back into focus. Where was I? I could hear running water. That brought some of it back. I could remember going under water, fighting for air. But I couldn't remember coming up again. I began to wonder if I'd died in that water. That would explain the light and darkness. People who came back to life after being officially dead always talked about trying to get to the light. The thought that I might be dead didn't scare me as much as I would have expected. I was too tired to care much one way or the other.

But then I crawled another step closer to full consciousness and knew I really was alive. Being dead couldn't hurt this much. . . . My whole body felt bruised and trampled —like all the times I'd ever been bucked off Spider had been rolled up together to make one giant ache. And my stomach didn't feel great either. It felt like I'd been throwing up for a week and could keep right on doing it the rest of my life.

But curiosity was getting stronger than pain. Somehow I had gotten out of the river. It might be worthwhile opening my eyes to find out how. I gave it a shot—but the hard glare of the bright afternoon sun slammed into my eyes like a fist. I closed them again fast, then turned my head a little and tried again. It was better this time. Something was blocking out the sun. No, not something. Someone. Kat? Kneeling there beside me on the sand, cradling my head in her lap? If I wasn't dead, I must be delirious. But I decided there were worse ways to be.

I lay still, too tired to move, and just stared up at her, wondering fuzzily how anybody who was wetter than a drowned muskrat, covered with mud, and wearing clothes a bag lady would have thrown away, could look so good. Red had always said she was beautiful. How'd he get to be so much smarter than me?

I still couldn't remember how I'd gotten here, and I would have asked her if it hadn't taken so much energy. She wasn't even looking at me. She was staring off into the distance talking to somebody. I wondered who. But then, all of a sudden, my brain unclouded enough for the words to start sinking in. . . .

"Please, God, don't let him die. I don't hate him. It wasn't his fault. I don't want him to die. Please . . ."

Wow! I could take hearing a lot of this. I'd done some pretty constructive eavesdropping in my day, and now it was real tempting just to lie there and take this all in. But listening in on somebody's conversation with God was different. It made me feel guilty—especially being the subject of the conversation. I decided I'd better quit playing possum while I still could. So I kind of accidentally-on-purpose coughed.

Instantly, Kat's eyes focused on my face, and even under all the streaks of mud, I could have sworn that she blushed. "How long have you been awake?" she asked accusingly. I couldn't decide which was stronger—Kat's relief that I really wasn't dead or her embarrassment at me knowing how badly she wanted me not to be dead.

"Long enough to know you don't hate me anymore," I said, my voice sounding like I'd swallowed all the gravel on the riverbed. She didn't answer for an awful long time.

Great, I thought. We just went through the shortest truce in history, and now she's mad at me all over again.

"Or do you?" I asked at last. Our eyes held for a long time. Then she sighed. "How can you hate somebody that just saved your life—sort of," she added, a smile just beginning to curl the corners of her lips.

I couldn't help smiling back. No matter what, Kat stayed honest. But she was right. It was "sort of." Because as far as I could remember, my great rescue attempt had ended up with me passed out in the middle of the river. From there on, it had all been Kat's show. And she never could read the script when it came to the part about how the guy's supposed to be the tough one. But thinking it over, I decided I liked being alive even better than I liked being macho.

Lying there looking up was making my neck hurt. I struggled to sit up—and that made *everything* hurt—but once my head quit spinning it wasn't so bad.

"So," I said, "how'd we get out of the river? Last thing I remember was reaching for a branch and passin' out."

Kat shrugged. "There wasn't much more. With you holdin' on to the tree, I just kept kickin' till I could get hold of it too. Then I pried you loose from that branch and worked my way along the tree until I could drag you out on the bank—"

"What do you mean 'pried loose'?" I interrupted. "I never did get hold of that branch. I tried, but that hand just wouldn't close."

Kat gave me a tired look. Then her eyes moved to my hand. "It wouldn't, huh?" she said.

I followed her gaze. My hand was lying at my side, relaxed, nothing special about that, except—I glanced up at Kat and then back at my hand—except that my fingers were curled lightly against my palm. Carefully, moving it like it might blow up or something, I raised my hand. It didn't look much different from before. Then I opened it. Slowly, sending pain throbbing up my arm, my fingers straightened. Just as slowly, I clenched my hand into a fist. I did it! It really worked. I had my right hand back.

I felt a huge grin spreading across my face. I looked up at Kit. "Did you see that?" I said. "It bends! It really does bend!"

"No kiddin'," she said in a bored, I-told-you-so voice. But she was smiling too.

I probably could have spent the rest of the afternoon just watching my fingers wiggle. I felt like a baby who's just made the startling discovery that his fingers and toes really do belong to him. But flexible fingers or not, it finally dawned on me that I couldn't just sit here for the rest of my life. I looked up to say something to Kat, and it hit me how pale she was. And her eyes, more gray than blue right now, had a haunted look. She'd been through hell in the last couple of days, I thought guiltily—and I'd been all wrapped up with my problems. Kat had to have more guts and determination than any girl—no, make that any *person*—I knew, but even she had a limit. And I figured she'd just about reached it.

"Kat," I said softly, "you okay?"

She didn't answer. She just turned those unbelievable eyes on me. And all of a sudden, I wanted to protect her from all the bad things in the world. I wanted to wrap her up and keep her warm and take her home and bring Uncle Joe back and . . . But I couldn't do any of it. All I could do was reach out and put my arms around her. If I'd have taken time to think about it, I might not have done that. I still had the claw marks on my wrist from the last time I'd dared touch her. But this time she didn't turn wildcat on me. She just breathed a deep sigh and laid her head on my shoulder. "It's gonna be okay," I whispered, brushing her long, wet hair back out of her eyes. "Just take it easy. Everything's gonna be okay." The words came real natural, almost like I'd said them before in another life or something. And then I remembered. I *had* said them, just last week—which might as well have been another life—to a horse that was real sick with colic. Life was starting to move way too fast for me.

I just sat there for a while, holding her. Then I heard her take a deep breath and she looked up at me. "Lance," she said, "I'm sorry."

"What for?" I asked, honestly puzzled. Right then I couldn't think of anything she had to be sorry about.

"You know what for," she said. "Everything. The way I've been treating you since . . . since the plane went down. You didn't deserve that. I know it wasn't your fault. I knew all along it wasn't. It was just that"—she swallowed— "that losing Dad, I . . . I couldn't handle it." Her voice went funny on her, and she turned away and stared into the distance. I knew why. She didn't want me to see the tears. She'd spent too long being tough and proud to break down now. I'd been down that same road, and I knew the feeling.

"Hey," I said gently, "it's okay. Go ahead and cry. You've got reason enough."

Suddenly Kat sat up a little straighter, and when she turned to look at me some of the old fire shone through the tears in her eyes. "Oh sure. Go ahead and cry, Kat," she said. "Sit right here in the mud and bawl your head off. That'll make everything better. That'll get us home. And while we're at it, maybe it'll bring Dad back too." She choked back a sob. "Just 'cause I'm a girl, you think cryin' is how I'm supposed to solve all my problems."

I sat there stunned. I felt kind of like I had four years ago when I'd accidentally torn that hornets' nest wide open. Kat was real steamed up about all this boy-girl stuff.

Only this time she had it all wrong. "Kat," I sighed, hardly realizing I was saying it out loud. "Bein' a girl don't have much to do with it."

"Yeah?" she said, a little defiance creeping back into her voice. "That makes a lot of sense comin' from you. Guys like you never cry."

I shook my head. "Wrong again, Kat. I've done my share in the last while."

"Over what?"

"My mom," I said, hardly believing I was telling her this. Kat gave me a puzzled look. "But Dad told me she left when you were five. Do you still miss her that much?"

I started to say no and then changed my mind. "Yeah," I said, "I do now. But I didn't so much before. I think her comin' back hurt more than her bein' gone."

"I don't get it."

"I wrote her out of my life, Kat. Pretended she was dead so it didn't hurt so much to think that she just took off and forgot all about me. But when she showed up after ten years, it kind of wrecked that theory." I broke off there. This was stuff I didn't talk about. Not even to Red—as he'd mentioned pretty clearly a while back. And now I was telling it to *Kat*? A couple of days ago I wouldn't even trust her with my horse.

But I just kept talking. Telling her stuff I hadn't even really known myself until I started putting it in words. Like the way I felt about my mom now.

"I want to see her again. I really do. But somehow after her tryin' to get custody and all, havin' anything to do with her makes me feel like I'm bein' disloyal to Dad. It's like, whatever I do, I'm havin' to choose between them." I went on for a long time and Kat just listened. Finally, I ran out of words—and energy.

Kat didn't say anything for a minute. Then she looked up at me. "We're pretty messed up, aren't we, Lancelot?"

"Yeah," I said, "you got that right." Reluctantly, I let go of her and stood up. "But, we're still gonna make it. Let's get goin'," I said, reaching out to help her up.

Kat scrambled stiffly to her feet. "So where do we go from here?" she asked.

I thought it was a pretty dumb question. Back to Red, of course. He must be going crazy up there alone. But before I had a chance to say that, a cool breeze drifted down the valley and sent a shiver up my spine. "The first place we're goin' is back upstream to find the rest of my clothes before I freeze to death," I said, rubbing my goose-pimpled arms.

Kat gave me a funny look. "Good luck," she said.

"What's that supposed to mean?"

"Look around," she said. "You want your clothes, you'll have to go swimmin' again. We came out on the opposite side of the river from where we went in."

For the first time since I'd opened my eyes, I really focused on the lay of the land. Kat was right. This was the *east* side of the river.

I stood there, feeling the last spark of energy drain out of me. All this. The crash, those miles and miles of rough country, the river that had tried to kill us. We'd made it through. We'd even made it through to each other. And for this? To be trapped on the wrong side of a flooding river with no food, no blankets, no matches, and another freezing night just hours away. This was it. I was giving up.

Kat shook back her hair. "So," she said, with just a hint of challenge in her voice, "why are we standin' here? You givin' up, Lancelot?"

I raised my head. " 'Course not," I said, managing to come up with a grin. "Upstream or down?"

Kat thought it over. "Down," she said, just like she was a tourist in Disneyland. "We've already been up."

"Okay, lady, anything you say." Another shiver ran through me. Kat noticed. She pulled off her torn jacket. "Here," she said, throwing it around my bare shoulders, "it's better than nothing."

"Hey . . ." I started to argue.

"Lance. . . ." Kat said warningly.

I sighed. Being macho dies hard—even when you're freezing to death. "Hey, uh, thanks," I said. Kat smiled. "Let's go," I said, holding out my hand—my *right* hand.

This time Kat didn't back up. She took my hand—gently—and we started downstream.

We stuck to the river—as close as we could, that is. But it was hard going. One minute we'd be practically walking in the river to find a passable trail. Then we'd hit a big jumble of rocks or a stand of willow too thick to get through and end up detouring completely out of sight of the water for a ways. It seemed like we walked a hundred miles in the next couple of hours, but I doubt if we'd really made much more than one mile downstream by the time the sun started sliding behind the big ridge to the west. It wouldn't be pitch-dark for a couple of hours yet, but it was getting cold. And we were on another detour, to get around a swamp this time.

We were just topping another little hill, and I was looking at the ground. Walking through rosebushes in your bare feet gives you that habit. Suddenly Kat's hand tightened on mine. "Ouch, watch it, huh?" I muttered. That hand was still plenty sensitive. Kat ignored my complaint. "Lance, look," she ordered. I looked. And I looked some more. How tired and cold and hungry did you have to get to start hallucinating, I wondered. And could two people have the same hallucination? Obviously Kat had seen it too.

There, huddled like a tiny town on the edge of the river, were about a dozen of those aluminum bunkhouse trailers you always see around oil rigs. This didn't seem to be an oil rig—at least there was no sign of a derrick—but it sure was something. It was pretty quiet down there though. I wondered where all the people were. Then the door of one of the trailers opened, and a man walked out. We started down the hill.

The man was a grizzled old guy with a big belly and a lot of gray stubble on his face. He watched, kind of mildly interested, as we came across the clearing at sort of a staggering run. You'd have thought that wild, half-drowned kids wandered into his camp on a pretty regular basis. He looked us over.

"Where's the other two?" he said, scratching his whiskery chin. We gawked at him. "Well," he went on impatiently, "aren't you the ones from the missing plane that this whole outfit's shut down to hunt for? You fit the descriptions of two of them, but there's supposed to be a pilot and a redheaded kid."

I took a deep breath. I was going to have to say this a lot of times in the next while. "The pilot's dead," I said, my voice not giving away my feelings, "but Red's up there." I waved vaguely to the southwest. "Across the river. Somewhere on this side of that big ridge up there." It didn't sound like much to go on, but the guy nodded. "Come on inside," he said, jerking his head toward the closest trailer. "I'll get on the radio to the chopper. It's out looking for you right now, but it's way too far north."

He did some talking on the radio while Kat and I collapsed into the nearest chairs and started working through a pot of coffee and a huge pile of sandwiches the man set in front of us. They'd obviously been meant for all those poor guys who were tramping around out there looking for us, I thought, feeling kind of guilty. But on my third cup of coffee, I stopped shivering enough to start getting curious.

"What is this place, anyhow?" I asked when the guy finished his radio work and came and sat down.

"Seismic crew," he said, not wasting words. "At least it was till this morning when some cop came on the radio with this big appeal for everybody out in northwest Alberta and northern British Columbia to help search for this downed plane." The man scratched his chin again. "I never did get it straight whether this guy's interest was personal or professional but, whatever it is, I've never seen a search this big organized this fast. He's got every off-duty cop in two provinces combing the woods too."

Kat and I looked at each other. I think we both had a

pretty strong suspicion who the cop might be and what his interest was.

Just then the radio crackled. The man answered it.

"Yeah," he said. "Sounds like the right general area. Okay. Good luck."

He came back. "Chopper pilot thinks he might have spotted smoke on a hillside over to the southwest. He's on his way to check it out. We'll know what he finds in an hour or so."

An hour or so turned into two hours, and still there was nothing from the chopper. We'd eaten all the sandwiches we could hold and drunk enough coffee to keep a truck stop in business. The old guy had even dug us up some soap and towels so we could at least wash off a little of the surface mud. But after that he settled himself at his desk with a pile of paperwork, and Kat and I just waited—and waited.

I had finally flopped down on a bunk, too tired to keep my eyes open, but I soon discovered I was too uptight to keep them closed. I was nothing compared to Kat, though. Just watching her pace that trailer like a newly-caged tiger was wearing me out. And I knew she was just as tired as I was. She had to be running on pure nerve. At last, I couldn't stand it any longer. I sat up. "Hey," I said. "That's not gonna help any! Come and sit down." I held out my hand to her. She sat down beside me and I put my arm around her, but I could feel the tension still running through her like electricity. "Take it easy," I said, softly. "Red's gonna be okay."

She looked up at me. "Promise?"

"Sure," I said confidently.

Come on, Paleface, I'm countin' on you, I said silently.

Suddenly Kat froze, listening. Then I heard it too. A faint egg-beater noise, coming nearer. . . .

Kat and I exchanged glances—and charged for the door just in time to see the helicopter settle in the clearing. Red didn't wait for anybody to help him. Before the blades had even stopped lazily flapping—fortunately, he remembered to duck—he was out of that chopper and limping over to meet us. I noticed that somebody had wrapped his ankle up in tensor bandages, which must have helped some. Anyway, right then I don't think he even remembered he had an ankle. A few feet apart, we stopped and stood looking at each other. We'd been separated maybe ten hours, but it seemed like a year.

It was Red who finally broke the silence. He looked from me to Kat and back to me. "You went *swimming* at this time of year?" he said incredulously, keeping his face dead serious. That crazy comment was all it took. Suddenly the three of us were together, laughing—or crying—by then I wasn't too sure what I was doing. I do know we all had our arms around each other.

Then our friend came out of the trailer. "Got enough gas left in that bird to haul these kids on down to Hinton, Charlie?" he asked. "He'll meet you there and pick them up."

I guess Charlie had enough gas. The next thing we knew we were climbing into the helicopter. I knew sort of where Hinton was, even though I'd never been there before. I didn't think I wanted to go there now. I just wanted to go home. But somebody was going to pick us up there. Maybe *then* we could go home.

I sat in the chopper and watched the treetops slide by underneath. I remembered reading somewhere that if something goes wrong with a chopper, it doesn't glide down like a plane does. When those blades stop whirling, it just goes down, splat, like an egg being dropped from the top of the Calgary Tower.

I don't know why, but that thought didn't even bother me. I was just too tired.

It was getting dark when we landed. I didn't pay too much attention to where we were, but I did notice the police car with all its party lights flashing come burning up to the chopper. Either this was the welcoming committee or, with the kind of luck we'd been having lately, we'd landed in a no-parking zone. Then I took a closer look at that car. It looked real familiar. It was the *Alderton* police car.

Before I had time to think any more, we were piling out and Red's dad was coming to meet us. "Dad!" Red yelled, and flung himself into the big cop's waiting arms. Kat and I stood back and waited. I heard her take a deep breath and swallow hard. This wasn't an easy scene for her to watch right now. I reached over and put my arm around her.

Red's dad was asking all the Are-you-all-right? questions and Red was answering them, but mostly they were just hugging each other to death. The lights on the cop car were still flashing. I saw them reflecting red, blue, red, off Red's dad's wet cheeks. I remembered Red out there in the hills saying, He'll never forgive me this time. Sure, Red, I thought, grinning in the dark.

Finally, Red's dad let go of him and came over to us. He gave us both a hug too. "I'm sorry," he said gently to Kat. He already knew. I was glad I didn't have to say it again.

A minute later he was all business. "Come on," he said, turning to help Red limp over to the car. "Your mom and Lance's folks are meeting us in Edmonton."

Edmonton? I was beginning to think I should have brought one of those little tourist gimmicks you get stamped in every different zone you visit. I didn't want to go to Edmonton. I wanted to go to sleep. Which I did in the car. As I drifted off, it occurred to me that Red's dad must be just as tired as I was. He was calling my dad "folks."

When I woke up we were just pulling into a parking lot somewhere. We stopped beside another car that had obviously been waiting for us—the lights were on and the engine was running. I didn't recognize the car, but it was Dad that got out. And Red's mom, and somebody else. A woman. At first I thought it might be Kat's mom. But it wasn't. It was the next day before she got things at home straightened out enough to get here.

I squinted into the lights, but I still couldn't see who it was. I got out of the car. Dad was standing there, waiting, like always. Not pushing himself forward, just there, ready when I needed him. And standing beside him . . . No, it couldn't be. I rubbed my eyes. My headache was back, pounding away behind my eyes. That must be why I couldn't see straight . . .

Then, "Welcome back, Lance," she said, and I knew I couldn't be imagining her voice too.

"Mom?" I couldn't get it to come out above a whisper. I started walking toward my mom and dad. For the first time since I was five I could walk toward one without having to walk away from the other. This time I didn't have to choose. But at the last second, I did choose. It was Dad I threw my arms around first. Because Dad had always been there—and I knew he always would be. He squeezed me so tight I couldn't breathe for a minute, and then he reached out his arms to Kat. I turned to Mom and, when I hugged her, somehow it felt right. This time she was more than a beautiful stranger who had showed up to mess up my life. "How'd you get here, Mom?" I asked at last.

"Your dad phoned me when he heard the plane was missing," she said, and I caught the look she gave Dad as she said it. That look said thank you a lot better than words ever could. Then she stepped back and looked at me. "Are you okay, Lance?" she asked, her eyes full of concern.

"Yeah," I sighed, letting my head fall back against her shoulder again. "I'm okay, Mom." And, for a change, I was telling the truth. I was more okay than I'd been for a long time.

25

We *still* didn't get to go home. That turned out to be a hospital parking lot and they dragged us all into the hospital for the night.

As usual, Red had been right. His leg hadn't been busted. He'd just tore a whole bunch of ligaments, which still didn't leave him exactly delighted at the beginning of basketball season. And Kat. Kat was all right. I knew she would be. Oh, the doctor said she was suffering from exhaustion, exposure, lacerations, contusions—neat words, huh?—and a pretty good case of whiplash from the jolt of the crash. But she was still all right. She was down at our room talking to me and Red so long that the nurse finally threatened to keep her in the hospital another night if she didn't get some rest.

I ended up with twelve stitches in my eyebrow—a fact that gave Red considerably more satisfaction than it did me. I got the doctor to check my hand too, but it was getting real late by then, and I don't think he ever really understood the whole deal. He wiggled my fingers back and forth—which was still no pleasure—and, between yawns, muttered something about how it seemed to be coming along fine and to just keep on with whatever therapy I'd been using on it.

Poor guy. When I broke out in crazy laughter, he just turned and walked away, giving me little backward glances all the way to the door. I don't think he was up to handling an all-out psycho at that time of night.

Well, from then on, things started slowly sliding back to sort of normal. Mom went back to Nashville after a few days. She had a concert tour lined up. I was sorry to see her go, but it didn't tear me up like last time. Because this time she and Dad said good-bye as friends. I guess maybe that doesn't sound like much to get excited about. Your parents are *friends,* living a thousand miles apart. But after a while you learn to accept what life gives you, instead of holding out for everything—and ending up with nothing. Besides, she was coming back at Christmas, and you could never tell. . . .

Kat's mom and her little half brother and sister came down and stayed for a couple of weeks.

It was good for us all to be together like that. Even though he'd never let on much, I could tell that losing Uncle Joe had hit Dad as hard as any of us. Sometimes he'd get real quiet—even for him—and just stand staring off at the mountains. I knew what he was thinking, but I couldn't think of the right thing to say. But Joey and Jessica, Kat's little brother and sister, didn't worry about what to say. In spite of being tore up about their dad, they were too young to stay down for long. They'd come tearing up and pounce on Dad like a pair of mousing cats and drag him off to take them riding or fishing or hunting for four-leaf clovers or . . . And that was all it took. Dad would be okay again. He's so crazy about kids—sometimes I feel kind of guilty for not being quintuplets.

And of course, no matter what else happened, Red and I had to go to school. We—well, mainly I—had some pretty serious catching up to do, and I'd finally decided on a few good reasons why it would be worth doing it. Kat helped me wade through old *Hamlet*—on top of all her other disgusting habits, Kat kind of *liked* Shakespeare.

But still, even though things were smoothing out on the

surface, I had this "unfinished" feeling all the time. Like there was something I really needed to do. The night before Kat and her family were going home, I figured out what it was.

I went up to my room real early that night. I said I had a headache, and since I'd had plenty of them since that crack on the head, it was a believable excuse. Believable to everybody except Kat. I felt her eyes follow me out of the room, and I knew she could tell I was lying. But I couldn't help it. What I was doing was for her. If it worked, she'd understand soon enough. If it didn't, I didn't want her to even know I'd tried.

I dumped all the stuff off my desk, got out my drawing pad and a charcoal pencil.

The next time I looked at the clock it was one in the morning. Crumpled papers filled the wastebasket and overflowed onto the floor, and my hand was so stiff and sore I practically had to pry the pencil loose from my fingers. But I'd done it. I stretched and leaned back in the chair and studied the picture in front of me.

Looking back at me was a big, strong face. A face framed with long black hair and a big black beard, and lit by laughing eyes and a come-and-get-me-world grin. The face of a man who'd died like he lived, unafraid and ready for the next adventure.

Technically, there was a lot wrong with the picture—that hand had a ways to go yet—but it didn't matter. Because the picture *was* Uncle Joe, and I was me again.

I gave Kat the picture the next day. And she cried. So did I. But afterward, it felt better. By the time we got to the airport, I knew we could handle saying good-bye.

Their flight had been called. Everybody else was heading for the gate. Kat and I stood there, looking at each other. Suddenly, I knew I wanted to kiss her good-bye, real bad. But *here*? It would be like those good-bye kisses in Grand Central Station in those old war movies. The whole *world* was watching. Still, I wouldn't see her again until Easter. It was going to be a long, cold winter . . .

Then there was Red. He wasn't even pretending to be minding his own business, and I figured he was reading what was on my mind as clear as if I'd advertised it in neon lights.

I wasn't so sure what *he* was thinking, but that look on his face was familiar somehow. Suddenly I recognized it. It was the look he gets in a basketball game when his team is down a few points, but he's a long way from giving up. I might have won the first battle, but I had a strong suspicion that the war for Kat had just begun. Which was one more good reason not to let this chance go to waste.

I still hesitated. This was going to take a lot of nerve. Kat was looking up at me with that old I-dare-you look of hers. Then somewhere in my head, a familiar voice spoke up: What's the matter, kid? You got cold feet? Go for it! And right then it didn't seem like Uncle Joe was gone at all.

Well, I hadn't had much practice at this, so I hoped it was like basketball—that I'd have a little natural talent. Anyhow, hadn't Kat always said I had more guts than brains? I leaned over, put my arms around her, and, real gentle, like she was breakable or something, I kissed her. And—she kissed me back! Just like everything else Kat ever did, *she* definitely had natural talent.

Reluctantly, I let her go and we stood there, staring at each other. "I suppose," I said, "you think you're better at that than I am, too."

Kat thought it over. Then she gave me her sassy grin. "I'll give you the benefit of the doubt, and we'll call it a draw—this time. But next time . . ."

Next time?

I figured Easter just might be worth waiting for.

Lose yourself in award-winning teen fiction from

Laurel-Leaf books!

___CAL CAMERON BY DAY,
    SPIDER-MAN BY NIGHT
    by A. E. Cannon 20313-9 $2.95

___CHARTBREAKER
    by Gillian Cross 20312-0 $2.95

___DUFFY'S ROCKS
    by Edward Fenton 20242-6 $3.25

___GROW UP, CUPID
    by June Oldham 20256-6 $2.95

___GUYS LIKE US
    by Stuart Buchan 20244-2 $2.95

___THE ISLAND KEEPER
    by Harry Mazer 94774-X $2.95

___THE WORLD IS MY EGGSHELL
    by Philippa Greene Mulford ..20243-4 $2.95

At your local bookstore or use this handy page for ordering:

DELL READERS SERVICE, DEPT. DFC
P.O. Box 5057, Des Plaines, IL. 60017-5057

Please send me the above title(s). I am enclosing $_____.
(Please add $2.00 per order to cover shipping and handling.) Send
check or money order—no cash or C.O.D.s please.

Ms./Mrs./Mr. _____

Address _____

City/State _____ Zip _____

DFC-8/89

Prices and availability subject to change without notice. Please allow four to six
weeks for delivery. This offer expires 2/90.